# D'Sire

BY

SYPREME ESSENCE

## Dedication

Thank You, thank you, thank you Universe for blessing me with this beautiful gift that I am able to share with the world. I am so grateful for all my family and friends that helped me get to this point in my life, please just know that it doesn't have to be written for you to know how much you all mean to me, and at the end of the day I hold each and every one of you close to me. Individually, you all help bring out the best in me, and help shape who I am today.

I am also truly thankful for all lessons learned through abrasive consequence that I had to endure because my head is hard. Ok God I get it. I don't have to be in incarcerated for my creative juices to flow.

Thank you Brian for opening this gate of opportunity for me, I appreciate you welcoming me into the King 4 Life family, my entry into this industry was not an easy task, there were several doors that were shut in my face, along with several people who used their power under the guise of professionalism not to help me but had their own ulterior motives. I owe much of my success to you and will always strive to put forth my very best work to make you proud. I thank you for your mentorship on the dos and don'ts of this industry and your time and patience that you've given me.

Mommy I just want you to know that you've played an intricate roll in my life that nurtured my ability to create all the wonderful characters in my mind. From the age of five I could remember always wanting to be by myself in my attic bedroom, surrounded by the comforts of everything that I loved, my books it was there where I taught myself how to read. There was one particular book that I was fascinated by, it was Peter Cottontail, a story about a fictional rabbit by Author, Thornton Burgess. It was a read -a- long book that came with the 45 record player that you bought me, and I just want you to know that you are the reason I write.

Davon, you are not only my oldest son you are my best friend. I gave birth to you at the age of 15, a baby myself having a baby. I did not know how to be a mother to you nor was I capable of teaching you the morals that you deserved, and as a direct result you were exposed to a life style that compromised your wellbeing, and you've suffered tremendously due to my actions. I just want to say that I am truly sorry for being so irresponsible, and that I am so proud of you because you developed your own value system, you grew up to be a beautiful person, and Davon you deserve the best that life has to offer. I hope that all of your dreams come true, and I love you beyond any expression of words.

Jahaad, the day I wrote this is special, because today is the day you called me with the news of getting accepted into Virginia State. Statistics said it wouldn't happen because you are the second of three children from a young, unmarried mother, who lived in the inner city. You too were exposed to my fast lifestyle, yet you chose not to conform to your environment. You remain an individual who is composed, extremely intelligent and highly driven to be the very best at whatever you put your mind to. Jahaad I want you to know that you make me proud and I know with all my soul that you will go all the way baby. My love for you is infinite.

Kilil, my baby boy. You are very special to me. I am so blessed to have you in my life. You were three weeks' shy of being born in prison, but through the grace of my heavenly father I was released just in time. It was during that period of my life when I realized I had a purpose. Just one year before you were born I almost lost my life from a gunman in a senseless act of violence. It was my personal wakeup call that I needed to change my life around. Although I've made several mistakes since then, you continue to strive for excellence, and I am extremely proud of you as well. You have a unique higher intelligence that the average child of your age does not possess, and you are so gifted with the ability to write music and poetry, and interpret the meaning of a philosophical view. You have a higher calling, and I am honored to be your mother my love.

Tito, ten whole years of age separates us, but I could remember like it was yesterday when mommy brought you home from the hospital, we lived in a small apartment in California. Those were some of the best years of my child hood because we were together. I don't know what happened but, when we moved back to Connecticut we became separated. I lived with grandma and you were with mommy. During those teenage years I fell in love with the streets when I should have been there for you, instead I was busy living a life which involved crime, sex, drugs and alcohol. At the age of five mommy moved you from Ct, and for ten years I cried because I longed to see your face so that I could be the sister to you that you deserved. I was supposed to protect you.

I am so thankful that we are back together again and that I get the privilege to see you raise your own beautiful daughter. I feel as though Nyla is you all over and that I am getting a second chance to teach her all the things that I was supposed to teach you as a child. I am so proud of you because you waited until you knew you were ready to have a child, and I know you are going to be the best mother a daughter could ever have, and I promise you that as long as I am here on earth I will always be there for you.

“Let me tell you something: from then until I left that prison, in every free moment I had, if I was not reading in the library, I was reading on my bunk. You couldn't have gotten me out of books with a wedge. Months passed without my even thinking about being imprisoned. In fact, up to then, I never had been so truly free in my life.”--- Malcom X

To my Incarcerated brothers and sisters hold your head up, your past does not define you.........

# Table of Contents

## Prologue

1990

"Grandma I'm sleeping in uncle Jr. room tonight." I sang as I skipped in to the kitchen where my grandmother sat in her favorite chair every evening before retiring to her bedroom upstairs.

"I keep having those scary dreams and uncle Jr. keeps the monsters away." I said in an angelic manner while twirling a lock of my jet black long tangled hair.

"Alright D'Sire did you take your bath?" My grandmother asked before taking a long drawn sip of her Folgers coffee.

"Yes grandma." I sweetly said batting my hazel green eyes inherent from my Puerto Rican mother. "Oh okay make sure you ask uncle Jr. if it's alright."

"I did he said it was ok just as long as I don't hog the covers like last time."

"Ok then baby don't forget to say your prayers."

"I won't."

"D'Sire, make sure uncle Jr. say his too." She added with a wink that made me giggle. "I will, you know I'm the boss of uncle Jr."

"I know you are baby goodnight."

"Goodnight grandma."

“That chile love her some uncle Jr.” I heard my grandmother say before rinsing her coffee cup and disappearing to her upstairs bedroom. I skipped steps down to my uncle Jr. room which was located in the basement of my grandmother’s brick house I loved it down there. It had its own kitchen and bathroom. Uncle Jr. let’s me do whatever I want when I’m down there. He even lets me eat all his snacks as long as I don’t tell grandma. I wrinkled my nose from the damp musky smell when I opened the door, and the darkness enveloped me. I navigated this course several times so it was easy to find uncle Jr. I tip toed in his direction and slid off my robe and Barney slippers that grandma gave me for Christmas, and climbed in the warm bed. Uncle Jr. was snoring but did not move. I whispered my prayers and my heart beat thumped hard in my chest. I could hear it cut through the stillness of the room. I curled up real close to uncle Jr. And fell asleep.

Several hours passed and I heard Uncle Jr. Whisper, “baby girl.” I did not answer pretending to be sleep. Uncle Jr. slid my purple Friday panties down and started to put his fingers in my stuff while he did something to his stuff.

“Damn baby girl I can’t wait till I’m able to stick it in you.” He whispered leaving a wet trace on my ear. Whatever that meant I wanted him to do it too. Uncle Jr. went under the covers and opened my little legs as wide as they would go. I could feel his warm tongue swirls all around in my stuff. This was a new game we played usually he would just touch my stuff and his stuff at the same time and put a sticky glob on my legs, but this time it was a much nicer feeling down there.

“This the best pussy I ever tasted.” Uncle Jr. never called it that before. The same noises uncle Jr. was making; I usually only make them in my head when he touches my stuff. But this time I could not hold them in. I wanted to show uncle Jr. that I loved whatever it was that he was doing. I began moving in uncle Jr’s mouth, humping my narrow hips which seemed to make him move his tongue faster and faster.

“Ohhh baby girl.” He moaned, making louder sucking noises down there. Uncle Jr. came up from the covers and I instinctively spread my legs for him. He put his pointer finger in my stuff. It hurt a little bit; he moved it in and out for a real long time.

“Baby girl I need to stick it in now cuz you ready.”

“Uncle Jr I’m scared is it going to hurt?”

“Don’t worry, it will only hurt for a little while until you get use to it then it will feel good.” He whispered. Uncle Jr instructed me to bite down on the pillow as hard as I could. I did as I was told and squeezed my eyes real tight as he put the top of his thing in me. I could feel my skin tear and it burned as he slowly inched it in. I cried and uncle Jr. covered my nose and mouth with his musty hand and I couldn’t breathe. My eyes bulged out of my head. Uncle Jr. humped me real fast and hard and my muffled screams went unanswered. I dookied on myself.

"Ooh baby girl this is uncle Jr. pussy now you bet not, never give it to nobody else or I swear to fuckin God I will kill you." Are the last words I heard before everything faded to black.

# CHAPTER 1

2010

Reluctantly I turned to face the stranger whose bed I occupied. I could not remember what he looked like and the darkness that engulfed the room was no help. His heavy breathing indicated that he was in a deep sleep. Careful not to disturb him I slowly slid the covers off my body. The scent of sex escaped its confined quarters.

"What the fuck did I do?" I mouthed and crept out the bed. "Oh shit!" As soon as I stood up a warm glob of sticky cum landed on my ankle. I searched frantically for my cell phone. I needed to get the fuck out there and vowed for the hundredth time never to pop ecstasy again. This isn't the first time I couldn't remember who I've fucked the night before and every six months the aids tests were getting so scary that I've become accustomed to holding my breath and clenching my midsection each time the results were read. I crawled on my hands and knees and fumbled around until I felt the wide shape of my BlackBerry curve under what appeared to be a pair of boxers. The flashing red light confirmed that it was indeed my phone. I pressed the little white ball and the screen illuminated the whole room giving me the advantage I needed to take peek of the complete stranger who obviously blew my back out.

I was quality pissed because his fool ass ain't even have the decency to strap his dick and even more mad at myself because my swollen pussy dripped with the remnant of his seed. Cloaked by the darkness of the room I crept to his side of the bed and again pushed the button of my cell phone. Damn this brotha was fine with his smooth chocolate self and still I wanted to choke the shit out of him. By the look of the room I could tell that we were in a half decent motel. There was a 35" black Magnavox flat screen mounted on the wall, a small white dorm refrigerator with an older microwave that sat on top and a red heart shaped Jacuzzi in the corner surrounded by mirrors. An empty fifth of Hennessey was posted between two clear plastic solo cups and our clothes were strewn everywhere. It seemed like I had a good time because there was no evidence that stated otherwise but still the night before was a hazy blur. My head pounded like hell and the after effects of the liquor had my breath doing kung fu.

I had to get myself together and the fuck out of here before this niggah woke up. Using my cell phone as a make shift light I managed to maneuver my way to the bathroom and closed the door behind me. The fan overhead came on as soon as I flicked the light switch so I quickly turned it off grabbed a wash cloth and complementary bar of motel soap and preceded to lather up my pussy with the hottest water I could stand. I dug in deep getting out as much as I could of the cum that invaded my insides. Although I've been through this scenario so many times, the feeling of utter disgust remains the same the moment it was time to wash away my sins.

The rapid tap on the door jolted me out of my trance of self-sabotaging affirmations.

"Are you ok in there?" A baritone voice of the stranger asked. Hesitating I answered.

"Yea I'm about to take a shower." I lied because I really just wanted to wash my ass real quick and bounce up out there.

"Can I join you?" He had the nerve to ask. Damn, I could have kicked my own ass. I felt for the light. No need to creep any longer because this niggah done woke up. Once again the fan rattled overhead, my eyes burned as they adjusted to the bright bulb of the track lights. I blinked hard as the image of myself appeared in the mirror before me. Even after a rough night of partying I still looked good so that wasn't the problem.

What lay ahead was far deeper I couldn't even recall the name of this niggah on the other side of this bathroom door. Think quick, think quick.

"I don't feel too well." I stammered turning on the shower. "I'll be out in a few."

"Well, could you at least let me in? A brotha got to piss."

"Damn!" I said while grabbing a white oversize bath towel before unlocking the door. I covered up.

"Thank you." The six foot something God said. He towered over the toilet with his muscular back towards me. I entered the hot shower. "Damn baby your sex is off da chain." He continued. I watched him through the frosted glass as he shook his huge dick and flushed. I stepped back from the spray in case the water got cold.

"You weren't too bad yourself." I answered back knowing damn well I didn't have a clue.

"Oh yea my bad the condom popped." He added while washing his hands. I breathed a sigh of relief.

"Yea I was worried about that too." I truthfully stated.

"I guess we both got caught up in the moment. I usually don't slip up like that."

"Me either." I lied ashamed of my truth.

"Next time we both need to be more careful." He added.

"Yea I know." I said in agreement. Wait did he just say next time?

"Well beautiful ima let you finish doing what it do and I'll see you when you come out aight."

"Ok." I said barely audible. A faint smile escaped my lips. I decide to play out the scenario a little while longer. After washing up I wrapped myself in the towel that I grabbed earlier and made my way into the adjacent room which was now well lit and clean. All my clothes were folded neatly in a small pile on the bed. My cream quilted Channel bag sat next to the carved initials ML♥LW on the wooden night stand. Inside the contents appeared undisturbed. Thankfully I always travel with tons of essential hygiene products. I had my share of situations such as these to know better. After brushing my teeth I strolled back to the bed and lotioned up with my favorite Dolce & Cabana lotion, Light Blue. With clean breath I was now ready to talk.

"Last night I was so fucked up of that e pill." I said.

"Yea, but damnnn you put it on me. We got ta do this again." He said with much excitement in his voice.

"Well if I had your number we could make it happen." I stated.

"212…" He began.

"Here, put it in my phone." He punched in the numbers and handed me back my cell.

"How do you spell your name?" I skillfully asked.

"Troy, T-r-o-y." He slowly recited.

"Oh that's easy" I blushed because it was obvious that I didn't remember his name. "Well Troy what are you getting into today?"

"I'm supposed to go to Harlem, meet with a few of my boys then head to the studio to finish laying down a couple tracks. What about you?" He asked.

"I'm going home to get some much needed rest then probably go chill with my cousin at her crib get fucked up, the usual." I blatantly lied trying to feel him out.

"Ima be back down here tomorrow I have to meet up with C.T. niggahs they sent me a demo and the shit is straight fire, then I'm performing at Toads Place in New Haven." He added a bit more animated.

"Oh really." I said, as my interest level in him kicked up a notch.

"Hold on bae I have to go to the car for a minute." He said making his way to the door. As soon as he closed it I jumped up and leaped to the window. This niggah was pushing a black on black chrome Bentley. A few minutes passed and he was back carrying extra clothes and toiletries in hand. "I'm always on the road so I come prepared." He said flashing beautifully kept teeth. Something was oddly familiar about him when he smiled. He was indeed a work of art. To best describe him he had smooth chocolate skin, chinky eyes and a 6ft something frame that was impeccably in shape.

I'm not the type to get all mushy over no niggah but in this case I just had to know more. As soon as Troy closed the bathroom door and I heard the spray of the shower I casually picked up his special edition BlackBerry and proceeded to scroll through the phone book and text messages. It didn't take long to figure out that the dude I fucked last night was not the average. He was R&B sensation T-Roy and it all started coming back to me how we ended up here. I was at the club with another niggah drinking and, rolling off ecstasy when I spotted Troy. I briefly remember sucking his dick in the men's bathroom and how we left together and almost crashed on the highway because I was fucking him while he drove. I nervously put the cell phone back in its respective place. All the whoring I've done finally paid off. Silently I gave thanks to the universe for placing me in the perfect time space sequence to meet this man. Several long minutes passed and T-Roy emerged from the steamy bathroom with a towel wrapped around his waist. Droplets of water kissed his beautiful body in perfect formation. I was truly in awe but tried hard not to show it. I didn't want him to know that I just discovered who he was by invading his privacy so I continued on as if nothing happened.

"I figure we could stop at the mall to get you a few things then grab a bite to eat before I bring you home. He said, unless you in a hurry."

"No hurry I'd rather chill with you for a bit longer if you don't mind." I casually threw back while scrunching my long tresses with my hands. My hair was now in its natural curly state due to last night's work out and me not wrapping it. I caught T-Roy staring at me through the reflection of the mirror.

"You look so sexy with your hair all wild."

"Thank you but I hate it. It's so unruly and hard to manage when it's like this." I stated clearly aggravated by the curly ringlets. Losing patience I just said, "Fuck it." While I threw it all up in a messy bun and hid behind my oversize black Leon Max sunglasses. T-Roy laughed. What you embarrassed to be seen with me?"

"No it's more like you being embarrassed with me looking like yesterday."

"Nawww Ma you the complete package I want you by my side no matter what you got on real talk. And I bet you don't even know that I'm one of your biggest fans."

"One of my biggest fans?" I asked with an open palm over my heart.

"Why so surprised ma? You are D'Sire, the columnist for Street Talk right?" He caught me off guard by knowing.

"Well yea but…"

"But what?" He cut me off. "You don't think your good enough for a fan base? All the industry cats know who you are and respect your writing game. You even got a niggah following you on Twitter, that's how I knew you were going to be at Club Image last night. I've wanted to get with you for a minute now and when the opportunity presented its self I jumped on it. I love that you're not all groupie out either and you know how to conduct yourself around celebrities. That's the type of girl I need on my team and it doesn't hurt that you give the best top a niggah ever had too". He added with a sexy devilish grin. I took no offence to what he said. I actually felt a sense of power over this man especially knowing that I left my signature trademark. Every time he touches his dick he gonna think of me.

## CHAPTER 2

Hitting up all my favorite stores with T-Roy was quite the exploit. Even with his blue fitted on and concealed behind Marc Jacobs aviators. He was still exposed. Fans flocked, taking pictures of us with their camera phones.

"Oh my God you will never believe who the fuck is standing in front of me right now!" A girl who looked around 12 yelled to the person on the receiving end of her jeweled out purple T-Mobile Sidekick. Our presence caused such a commotion that we had to be police escorted to each store. Jealous bitches slit their eyes and threw salty attitudes in my direction. Unfazed, T-Roy and I still walked hand in hand.

"Looks like you just made a few hundred enemies." T-Roy joked.

"Oh well let them hoes deal with their feelings." I replied with a slight neck roll.

"Oh shit, let me find out I got my own personal body guard". He joked further.

"Yupp and I'm going to protect you from all the haters." I said.

"Oh really now I definitely got at keep you around." He said and kissed my forehead. My solar plexus fluttered, releasing a flow of warm energy throughout my body that I've never experience before. I've been getting dicked down since the age of five and learned how to detach myself from my body when my uncle would fuck me and every niggah after him.

So why was this one different? My pussy got wet from the thought of my uncle and it made me so furious that I couldn't control the urge to fuck random dudes now that he's dead but at the same time I was a fiend for dick and it was my uncle who unleashed the demon sex goddess that prowled within me.

Our trip to the mall was much longer than anticipated. Between T-Roy posing with fans and signing autographs it was becoming exhausting.

"Let's slide up out of here and next time I will make it up to you. We could hit up some exclusive stores in the city where we won't be bombarded and you can pick out whatever you want aight." He assured.

"Okay that's what's up." I said giving him a sexy smile. The police continued to escort us through the mall all the way to T-Roy's car and mall security carried our bags. We genuinely thanked them before pulling off. I watched screaming fans become smaller in the side view mirror as we exited the parking lot and turned onto the main street. I let out sigh of relief that didn't go unnoticed.

"Welcome to my world ma. You ready for all this?"

"I was born ready. I take whatever life throws at me keep what I want and throw the rest right back." I caught myself say. I could only imagine how many other women T-Roy does these things for and claim as his own but none of that mattered to me because I had the chess game in life on smash. I knew how to play it all too well and I had to keep in mind that even though T-Roy was a star I was the one who controlled my world and he was just a visitor.

T-Roy pulled over "Drive Ma." We switched seats. He pushed some code on the LCD screen on the console and suddenly my seat began to move. It adjusted itself to the perfect height and length of my body as if it personally knew me. Jay-Z's Blue Print III album cover appeared on the screen.

Troy punched in some more codes and Death of an Auto Tune began to flow out the Infinity Speakers that surrounded us. It only took us about 25 minutes to reach the outside gate of my condo I flashed my Id card at the camera and the gate slowly opened allowing us to enter. I parked right next to my white 320 Mercedes Benz coupe.

"That's you ma?" T-Roy asked pointing at my car.

"Yea how did you know?" I asked really wondering because my car is not posted on Twitter.

"I could just tell; it fits your style." He said throwing a side compliment. For some reason I wasn't buying that one but decided to leave it alone. We sat idle for a brief moment.

"So Troy would you like to come up? I could make you something. We got side tracked with all that going on at the mall we didn't get a chance to eat and I am starving so I know you got to be."

"You sure ma? I don't want your boyfriend coming home kicking doors down n shit."

"Niggah I'm single and if you follow me on Twitter like you said you do then you would know this already."

"There goes that attitude that I love again." He said with a wink.

"Well then come on." I said. T-Roy popped the trunk and grabbed all my bags. He secured his car with the alarm and we headed up the four marble stairs that led into the elegantly styled elevator lobby.

"Hold on Troy let me check my mail." I hurried to the mail room and was back in a flash.

"Anything for me?" T-Roy joked.

"Yupp." I replied. "A whole bunch of bills." We both laughed. I felt overly confident inviting him inside my condo because I just had my white carpet professionally shampooed and my crib was immaculately clean and tastefully decorated with contemporary high end furniture.

The elevator bell chimed at the 13th floor and the mirrored doors parted. A short walk down the plush carpeted hallway led us to my abode. The scent of honey vanilla Glade plug INS welcomed us as we entered. Immediately I took of my Prada shoes while T-Roy followed suit.

"Where do you want these?" He questioned holding department store bags up.

"Oh my bad I'll put them in my room. Thank you so much Troy, I appreciate these things very much."

"Your welcome bae." I heard him say before I disappeared into my lavish bedroom. I placed each article of clothing in its perspective home then rejoined T-Roy.

"Make yourself comfortable, the remote is on the coffee table it controls the stereo and the TV so you may take your pick." I said.

"I love how you live ma."

"Thank you." I knew as soon as he spotted my fish tank coffee table I would get some type of reaction from him. I smiled inward because I knew he was used to having all the finer things that life had to offer him. But so was and even though my money was not as long as his you would not be able to tell because I lived way over my means. My professional writing career did afford me the basic luxuries. But I took basic to a whole new level. My motto is simple if I'm going to be about money I have to live like money and only surround myself around the winners. No time to second guess myself or weigh options I just got to do it like Nike said and that's how I live. Even when I leased this condo I didn't bitch about the price. I knew it would be a grip because of its beach front and breath taking views. It was closest to what I've envisioned, which is a Manhattan sky rise overlooking the Hudson. T-Roy opts for the Lakers game which projected from the 52" Sony flat screen mounted on the wall.

"Troy do you want something to drink? I have bottled water, Orange juice, Pepsi, Heineken and…"

"I'll take a Heineken ma" I decided on one too. I opened our beer and handed T-Roy his. I poured mine in a glass.

"Troy do you eat pork?" I just had to ask because it seems as if every man I meet is on some Muslim kick."

"Yea, what you making?"

"I was thinking about something quick but feeling like some double bacon cheeseburgers with sauté onions and peppers, sweet potato fries on the side and a garden salad. Unless you prefer Caesar. And don't worry I have plenty of mouthwash and an extra toothbrush."

"Damn baby you throw down in the kitchen, blazing in the bed and know how to take care of me let's just skip the ceremony and head straight for the honeymoon." Troy had me cracking up. After the burgers cooked I placed them on the warming tray and covered them to keep the juices sealed in. T-Roy stood behind me while I prepared the salad and kissed the back of my neck.

The sensation sent pulsing waves first up then down my spine I closed my eyes and silently mouthed, "Thank you." To the universe and continued to savor the moment. T-Roy slid his hands down and around to the front of my Seven Jeans. He released the button and zipper all in one fluid motion. I sucked in a breath as his strong yet gentle hand found its place upon my treasure. He began to massage the plump folds of flesh in a circular motion. I bit my bottom lip. My pussy instantly swelled, over lapping his fingers.

I slowly began to grind my hips. Troy turned me around to face him, slid my jeans and removed the black Fredrick's thong that I changed into down lifting my feet one by one out of them and hoisted me on the counter. I tilted my body until the arch formed in my back I supported the weight of my body with my hands against the counter. T-Roy lifted my legs on his shoulders and dove in. His tongue beat rhythm upon my pussy like an African on a new drum. My legs shook and I screamed his name as I climaxed. Troy lifted me off the counter.

"Let me hit it from the back bae." He said while stepping out his Roca wear Jeans and boxers. The thick vein in his huge dick pulsated and precum expelled from the perfectly shaped helmet head. I assumed the position and allowed him to enter me without protection. The back shots that T-Roy gave sent my soft thick ass into a rippled frenzy as it slapped against his swinging balls.

"Oh I love this pussy oh my God baby I love this pussy." Hearing that familiar chorus made me throw the ass back, reciprocating each of his moves with a counter reaction of my own. We were in perfect rhythmic motion and our steamy sex scene was orchestrating a divine dance right here in my kitchen in front of an audience of stainless steel appliances. It was unbelievable. We kept on in that position for about 20 minutes and somehow made it to my bedroom upon my pillow top mattress where I rode the life out his dick and put his ass to sleep for about two hours. Then woke him up to a dick sucking he would never forget. We showered together and ate the food that I prepared. It was so obvious that he was comfortable and didn't want to leave. Every now and then he would check his messages and text the person back and return a call if it was important enough. I could clearly see that he was the one in charge by the conversation I overheard him having with his manager.

"Sometimes this music shit gets real aggravating mutha fuckas act as if I don't have a life outside of my voice. They act as if they can't function if I'm not present. What the fuck do I pay these people for if I have to be around 24/7?"

He was clearly heated I kissed his lips, "Troy I understand the stress you must be under and I want you to know that I'm here for you. Anytime you feel the need to escape it all, my door is open." I genuinely expressed. Troy hugged me tight.

"Thank you baby you give me a sense of normalcy I'm free to be me, not T-Roy the celebrity but Troy the human being. I had a good time D'Sire and would love to see more of you. After I handle my B.I. ima be back down here tomorrow to check these niggahs and perform three songs. On my way down I could scoop you, then after the show we could head back my way."

"Ok sounds like a plan. That gives me some time to catch up on a couple of article assignments and Tweet my readers. I've been off the scene for a whole 24hrs and I know they are dying to know what I've been doing." I said.

"I'll be here around 5:30. I know that's early but I have to do a sound check on my way ok." T-Roy kissed me slow and deep. Then walked out the door. I smiled to myself because I knew from this day on my life would never be the same.

## CHAPTER 3

T-Roy picked me up on time as promised. I was sure to be turning heads tonight with my tight black leather Valentino pants that rode my ass like a second skin, sexy sleeveless low cut top that showed the perfect amount of cleavage and chrome Jimmy Choo criss cross stilettos. I accessorized my arm with a platinum diamond oyster shell face Chanel J-12, adorned my neck with a diamond and onyx choker while 2 carat GI certified flawless, princess cut diamond earrings dripped from my ears. My black Valentino clutch complimented the whole ensemble and my hair was in a classic up do ballerina bun held with genuine Swarovski crystal covered chop sticks that were custom made for me as a birthday gift from the editor in chief of the magazine I write for.

I just wanted to represent T-Roy to the fullest and etch an impressive image of me in the heads of his counterparts. "Damn baby you look beautiful." T-Roy said as he stepped out of his car holding the aura of a king, he rocked a pair of black Giorgio Armani slacks with a form fitted shirt that showed off his impeccable physique and a pair of black on black Stacey Adam alligator shoes. His Presidential diamond Rolex dazzled along with the diamond incrusted chain and cross that stopped right above his navel. The pulse of street fashion combined with a twist of high end was timeless.

"Look at you getting your sexy grown man on." I said to him as he walked to my side of the car. T-Roy wrapped his arms around my small waist and pulled me close to him. The exotic scent of his Jean Paul Guiltier cologne was extremely intoxicating. He held my chin and kissed me. His full luscious lips consumed mine and I gently bit his. Instantaneously my nipples became hard and my pussy began to awaken with her own heartbeat. I just wish he would say fuck everybody and dick me right here. I wanted him inside me so bad.

The thought soon dissipated because I know that I wasn't dealing with the average man. T-Roy had a prior commitment that he was getting paid big paper to fulfill and I knew better than to think he would allow my pussy, no matter how good it was to get in the way of his livelihood. The niggah T-Roy was supposed to meet sent him a text with directions to where they would be. I was familiar with the area; I just wouldn't classify it as a specific side of town or anything but others would just say that it's RT 80 off exit 8. T-Roy text back saying that we were on our way then opened my door in a way that made me feel special. I snuggled perfectly into the buttery soft tan custom leather seat of the white Mercedes Benz s 500. T-Roy entered on the driver's side and punched the address in the navigation system then he hit a code on the LCD screen similar to the one in the Bentley and Donnell Jones Journey of a Gemini album cover appeared and the first track began to play.

"Oooo you don't know how much I love this CD." I said with the biggest smile ever.

"Oh yes I do." He said before driving off.

"Let me guess another Twitter moment right?" I asked really curious to how he knew. He didn't answer but his ear to ear grin told it all. T-Roy found the street with ease. Since we took the highway it only seemed like about a 20-minute ride from my spot. When we arrived T-Roy parked behind an older black Yukon Denali in front of a small but nice ranch style house with modern windows and new beige aluminum siding. Three guys who all looked to be in their early twenties emerged from the house onto the porch. Out of the three one in particular caught my eye. He was tall and brown skin. He wore a pair of dark blue, Roca Wear jeans with red stitching, a long white tee and red white and black retro Jordan's. His low cut showed off swirls of jet black wavy hair and his edge up was crisp. The brotha was fine. The other two niggahs were average looking they both were light skin with good hair. One had on a long gold Cuban link chain with a microphone that reached past his solar plexus, baggy LRG Jeans, a long white tee and some white uptowns.

And the other had on a pair of Rocawear sweat pants, a long white tee and some black, white and red Jordan's he rocked a Miami Heat fitted and a had a basketball in his hand with the word Spalding written in cursive across it.

"I like these cats they are all about business they don't have a whole bunch of niggahs hanging around the house." T-Roy said with a look of relief. T-Roy exited the vehicle and popped the trunk. He took out a Gucci portfolio along with a whole stack of CD's and walked to my side of the car and opened the passenger door, like a perfect gentleman he took my hand to help me out. T-Roy closed the door behind me and we walked hand and hand across the paved path that led to the porch. T-Roy introduced each of the guys one by one by their governments and street names to me giving them pound and a brotherly embrace. The one I was attracted to name was Tyrell, T.Y. for short we locked eyes for a brief moment and out of respect for T-Roy he broke his stare first. T-Roy and I were led to the side rear of the house to a small modern shed like structure that matched the exact same color of the house. It was quaint, almost cottage like. It had a small window with white shutters on each side of it, a white door with a screen and a green welcome mat that sat in front of it.

Marcus, the one that had the basketball earlier opened the screen, unlocked the door and threw the keys to the other light skin dude, Rick. Once inside I realized this was a make shift studio. I could tell these guys took a lot of pride in what they did. This place had all the amenities of a major industry studio minus the luxury. Right above the black leather sofa on a cranberry colored wall was a professionally painted logo in black cursive letters that read Big Mouth Records. Opposite of that there was framed certificate that proved the legitimacy of this business as a LLC and right next to it was their mission statement. Grey foam egg crate aligned the walls of the built in sound booth and through the Plexiglas window I saw a tall silver professional stand up microphone with a spit screen attached. Where the engineer sat there was two flat screens one 13" the other about 19" they were hooked to a computer, Pro Tools on the screen and some kind of mixing board that flashed red, green and yellow lights. In the corner was a professional Sony key board that sat on a black stand and a shiny wood grain acoustic guitar.

I played my position in the cut. I was happy to see a few Street Talk Magazines on the side glass table. Pretending to flip through a recent issue of Dons & Divas. I overheard T-Roy giving sound advice to the guys about the industry.

"First and foremost you must hire a consultant, attend the annual DJ conference and you have to invest in yourself through marketing, if nobody knows who you are but you and your team then you ain't going nowhere."

"About a month ago we sent a professionally mixed cd to the station here in CT and they still haven't played our music on the radio and I know that our shit is what CT needs to be put on the map, but these radio niggahs won't even give us a chance." Rick protested.

"Besides the cd what did you give the station?" T-Roy asked.

"Nothing," Rick answered.

"Then what do you expect? Nothing equals nothing all day. Don't expect the radio stations to support you if you're not supporting them it's all a numbers game when it comes to this music shit." T-Roy said. "These radio stations receive demos everyday seven days a week. I'm pretty sure that some of them are fire, but the only thing that matters is what makes your stand out. And I can tell you right now it's not the graphic design on the cd cover or the paper the bio is printed on. It's far deeper than that. Let me ask you a question Rick; where do you work?"

"At Hat Land in the mall you know the store that sells all the latest fitted, that's where I got this one from." He proudly stated showing off the authenticity of it. "Why haven't you taken the time to Google the radio DJ's and find out their favorite teams or colors? By investing in yourselves you all could have collectively bought about a dozen hats and sent them along with your cd. Nobody's going to turn down a crisp fitted, but the main thing is you get your music heard." T-Roy said.

"Damn I never thought to do that. Rick said.

"Nobody ever does that's why you have to be creative when it comes to this shit." T-Roy reiterated. For the rest of the time we spent T-Roy lent his vocals on consignment for the hook on a track he liked. From his portfolio he pulled out a professional contract that was drawn up from his lawyer that stated if any profit was made from the sale of this song, then T-Roy would receive and undisclosed percentage that was between the label and him. T-Roy advised the guys to hire a lawyer of their own to go over the contract but out of anxiousness they hastily declined.

## CHAPTER 4

I love down town New Haven CT especially right now because its summer. When the sun retires for the evening Yale's Majestic historic campus buildings tower, casting eerie shadows of mysterious wonder. A host of specialty shops surround the area and a multicultural sea of happy people from all walks of life patronize the bistro bar & grilles to the capacity. Couples who prefer a more intimate setting will grab an outside votive candle lit Iron umbrella table to enjoy drinks and a tasty meal in the soothing warm breezy air.

T-Roy made a right turn onto York St. "Good my DJ and media man is already here." He said while parallel parking his big bodied Benz in the reserved spot that awaited him. An average looking middle aged clean shaven, Caucasian man wearing a green T-shirt with white letters that said Toads Place and faded denim American eagle jeans came out to greet us with his hand extended.

"Hey T-Roy what's good my man?"

"What's up Bo, this is my beautiful girl D'Sire." T-Roy proudly stated while introducing me. "And that she is a true beauty. You're a lucky man T-Roy." Bo stated with admiration in his voice.

"Why don't the two of you come with me." he said as he opened the door then led the way. There were a few square wooden tables scattered in the first room we walked in and a small leveled wall divided one side from the other room which was much bigger. This is where you will be performing T-Roy. Bo said as we walked into the bigger room. It was very spacious even with the stage you could tell that it held a pretty decent sized crowd. T-Roy's DJ was busy setting up his equipment.

"What up my niggah!" T-Roy yelled upon entering. T-Roy's DJ jumped down from the stage. They embrace and gave each other pound. A painfully thin tall young tan white woman walked up on us and offered drinks. I ordered a glass of Moscato, T-Roy and his DJ Heinekens and Remy. The media man emerged from behind the stage with a Nikon camera strapped around his neck carrying a zoom lens in his hand. He carefully placed the lens inside a black leather padded case with white stitching and set his tripod stand up in the corner before joining us. He declined a drink. T-Roy introduced me to DJ Infinite and his media man Jerome as his girl. I thought he slipped up earlier and said it when I met the owner Bo but wasn't sure I heard correct. This was a confirmation that I did. So I guess I was for the night.

We all followed Bo past a fully stocked bar to a stairwell that led to the basement. Once down there we walked a long corridor to a private room. Inside was a large buffet. On silver warming trays were a variety of wings Swiss meatballs and dipping sauces. Next to that was a table with platters of exotic fruits and cheese, an assortment of Melba toast, crackers, dips and a few trays of garden vegetables. Several buckets of expensive champagne sat on ice strategically placed around the room. The people who set this room up must have thought T-Roy traveled with an entourage because it was way too much food for just us four. Adjacent to the room was a smaller private quarters inside just a king size bed and my imagination went bananas just off the thought of what goes down in that room. DJ Infinite and T-Roy were fully engaged in an animated conversation. You could tell that they were close and knew each other for a long time. The white woman who took our order returned with drinks on a small brown tray. T-Roy thanked and gave her a hundred-dollar tip. He also autographed her cd. The woman openly flirted with him in front of me it was obvious that she acted differently when her boss wasn't around. I wasn't fazed by it all actually I thought it was quite entertaining. Jerome, DJ Infinite whos government is Shawn and I made small talk.

"D'Sire where you from?" Asked Shawn.

"Right here in Connecticut, Bridgeport native I answered."

"Ok that's what's up no wonder why you so down to earth. You got any friends that look like you?" Jerome asked.

"Nope don't do the friend thing besides my job is demanding I'm always on assignment so I don't really have a lot of free time unless it's of benefit to myself."

"Oh really. What's your field?" Jerome pried.

"Journalism, I write for Street Talk Magazine."

"Oh shit I read that publication on the reg, matter of fact that's one of the hottest magazine's out in the industry right now." He said.

"Ok ma I know who you are now. I'm very familiar with your work you are a very talented writer. Maybe if you don't mind we could do some work together. I have a few projects coming up and I need a ghost writer."

"Ok that's something to think about I love to expand my creative source." I said with a smile. We exchanged numbers. I became genuinely happy anytime I spoke about my passion somehow I felt that through these synchronized events that were presenting themselves to me, held the key to a much greater purpose and the universe was indeed moving mountains for me.

"You got my girl over here all smiling what you trying do bag her?" T-Roy joked.

"Nawww man we just kicking it."

"You got a very beautiful gifted woman here I was just telling her about the project that me and you discussed about a month ago and that I could use her help with." Shawn said.

"Oh you talking about that performing arts center project." T-Roy said.

"Yea remember I was saying that I needed a writer for the proposal, someone with that creative glitch that could translate my vision into words."

There was a knock at the door, "Come in." Jerome and T-Roy both said at the same time.

It was the owner Bo, "Hey T-Roy it's time for sound check."

"Aight man we'll be up in a couple of minutes. T-Roy answered.

"Ok buddy. Is everyone comfortable? Do you guys need anything?" Bo asked.

"No thanks Bo we are fine. Just give me a moment." Shawn and Jerome took that as their Q to leave. As soon as the door closed T-Roy and I shared silence for a moment before he spoke.

"D'Sire I aint going to front you got me open baby. I know we just practically met but for some reason I feel so connected to you. I know you been hearing me all night long introducing you to my peoples as my girl. I hope that did not offend you."

"No offense taken, you see I rode with it. We just need to take this slow and allow the feelings to build up and see where it goes. Speaking for myself, I enjoy being single because I love the freedom of not being tied down and plus before I do settle I need to know that I've made the right decision and even more that I'm ready." I said with sincerity in my voice.

"I respect that ma, but it doesn't change how I feel about you." I took in every syllable of the words this man spoke and tucked them away. T-Roy hypnotized the crowd with his soulful voice and tantalizing lyrics. Beautiful model like females of all races fought to claim their spots in front of the stage all in hopes of being serenaded. When he belted out the chorus of his hit single Lonely Star some of the women had to be carried out the establishment for fresh air. Others brazenly flashed titties and ass hoping to get bagged for the night. It was all so unreal. I could not believe the extent one will go just to get close to a celebrity. It felt good to be chosen and not have to compete for T-Roy's attention. Tonight I reigned supreme over the masses.

I tweeted my followers giving them a back stage pass into my world for the night before signing off. It was important to keep my readers updated on my where a bouts and an inside glance into my daily life. To this day I still don't know why they care so much but they do. I guess the blogger's world of modern technology is just another form of addiction people lose their soul to. Everybody from the family pet to the president of the United States is doing it. After performing the last of his songs, T-Roy placed the microphone back on the stand and thanked his screaming fans. He stood on stage for a moment taking in the energy of the crowd. He thanked them again before exiting the stage.

"How did I do?" He asked smiling knowing already what my answer would be. So I threw in a curve ball.

"How about you let me show you later. I whispered in his ear then kissed him on the check lightly brushing my hand across the front of his pants I felt the rise in his dick. I was well aware of my surroundings so I knew it wasn't going down in here not with all these people around and was not too keen on seeing our sex tape all over U-tube, so I decided to stay composed yet anxiously anticipated what the rest of the night would bring.

## CHAPTER 5

We said our goodbyes to Bo, Jerome and Shawn. With security in tow, we made our way to the conspicuous door that led to the outside where T-Roy's Benz was. The warm breezy night air kissed my face and it felt so good to be released from the stuffy confines of the bar. Once inside the car we safely watched behind the dark tinted windows as the groupies assembled themselves around the outside perimeter of the bar waiting for T-Roy or second choice, any baller to emerge from the door. They fixed their hair, jacked up skirts and overly exposed cleavage in hopes to score big for the night all for bragging rights to their friends. T-Roy turned to me and stared in my eyes intensely. "What?" I said slightly embarrassed so I giggled.

"Nothing I'm just admiring how good you look." He answered.

"What's on the agenda for the rest of the night T-Roy?"

"Me, you and my place." He said flashing brilliant whites. T-Roy's cell phone rang. The sudden look of disgust displayed across his face was an indication, to me that the call was unwanted. He sent the person directly to voicemail. Whoever it was didn't let up easy, calling aback to back until he put the phone on vibrate then silent. I didn't feel as it was my place to ask questions so I left it alone but I did make a mental note. His attitude was slightly different when we pulled off. 95 South was congested with traffic from weekend commuters looking for an escape to the city that never sleeps, New York. I decided not to allow that caller to deter me from having my own good time tonight either. T-Roy still appeared to be disturbed by it and his body language seemed quite tense so I decided to give him something to ease his mind a lil bit and regain focus on the prize that was present. I began to un do his pants. He willingly rose up so I could slide them down along with his boxes. I lifted up the butter leather arm rest that separated the driver's seat from mine. T-Roy's big dick started to rise, subliminally sending signals for me to perform the tango with it, my mouth as the stage. I took his swollen member and gently grasped it in my right hand and bought it to my plump soft lips allowing just the head to enter and butterfly licked under the rim of it with my tongue then began a rhythmic suck while I took the rest of him deep throating as I glided my hand up and down his thick shaft. Several moans of passion escaped T-Roy's clenched teeth as he grabbed the back of my head in attempt to control my pace that already had him swerving in his lane. I continued to tongue worship my king warrior Mandingo as if it guaranteed me a permanent spot in the afterlife.

"Oh my God baby I'm about to cum I'm bout-to-cum." He chorused 15 minutes into my sucking frenzy. I allowed him to expel his seed in my mouth and spit it out in a wad of tissue he had stored in the glove compartment. The wind whirled in causing me to squint as I let down the automatic passenger side window to toss it out the car and handed T-Roy some extra so he could wipe off too.

"Damm D'Sire, I can't put into words what you do to me." I just smiled at him and reclined my seat back enjoying the ride and music the rest of the way. We crossed over the George Washington Bridge that led into Manhattan. The city's lights memorized my soul as they danced flickers across the skyline. I closed my eyes to absorb the energy that the city was sending me through confirmation that everything I've envisioned was on its way. T-Roy pulled up in front of his Park Avenue sky rise. The clad dressed valet with sparkling blue eyes like razors opened my door and greeted me.

"Good evening ma'am." T-Roy handed over his car keys. "Good evening sir." The valet said after graciously accepting.

"Thomas how many times do I ask you to just call me Troy."

"I know Troy sir but I'm not supposed to." He nervously stammered.

"Who's going to tell Thomas? We have this conversation every day."

"Yes sir." T-Roy just smiled and shook his head. I thought it was one of the funniest things I've ever witnessed. The doorman held the heavy glass oaked framed door allowing us access in to the grand foyer of the breath taken lobby.

"Good evening T-Roy and Miss Lady." He appeared much older than the valet.

"Hey what's good Leroy my man?" T-Roy said giving him a firm handshake. "Wish me luck Leroy I'm trying to make her my girl." Leroy flashed me a genuine smile. I shyly smiled back. T-Roy always seemed to know how to make me the center of attention in a way that made me feel special. The beautiful crystal chandelier hung over us in brilliance as the light it casted was the equivalent to grade A.G.I. certified diamonds giving off the impression of royalty. An exotic bouquet of sweet smelling flowers sat in grandeur upon a golden pedestal in front of a mirrored wall opposite of the elevator, which we took to the 37$^{th}$ floor. There was a woman who closely resembled Beyonce' waiting as the doors opened.

"Hello T-Roy." She smiled and said.

"Hey Nyjah." T-Roy replied. "This is D'Sire we both gave counterfeit smiles. *Another mental note*. She entered after allowing us to exit first. "See you later." She managed to low ball before the doors shut. I pretended not to hear. I was not going to give T-Roy any indication that I was the least bit jealous of her. Once a niggah senses jealous tendencies it's a wrap. He will always use it against you as the weapon of choice and will ultimately destroy you with it sending you into a downward spiral where eventually you began to question yourself worth and start to look for the opinions of those who do not matter to validate who you are. I took a vow early in life never to become that statistic. T-Roy's apartment was everything I envisioned a Manhattan sky rise to be from its roaring floor to ceiling windows with majestic views of the city to the roof top terrace where the elite came out to play. His furniture was retro mod there was a white couch with black and red solid pillows that went the whole length of it. An authentic zebra skin rug that lay on pure white carpet with a red art deco plastic table in the shape of sideways S. The art displayed on the walls was all authentic abstract paintings on white canvas. His 60" something flat screen by a Japanese name I could not pronounce hung on the opposite wall of the couch above a black marble fire place. The kitchen was every chef's dream it seem to connect to the living room all decked out in chrome and red. Everything matched from the pots that hung over the black marble island on the metal rack to the appliances in those same colors.

I've never seen anything like it, just absolutely gorgeous. There were two bed rooms. We by passed the first one the door was closed and I didn't bother to ask why. Ok the master bedroom was to die for everything in this room was chrome black and mirrored. The massive king size bed had four towering black leather post with a matching leather headboard. There was two mirrored walk in closets I assumed his and hers. One closet had all his shoes and sneakers and accessories such as his ties, belts and hats.

The other one had all his clothes everything was either neatly folded or hung up and color coordinated. The master bathroom was adjacent to the room. It had a black marble shower big enough for six people with overhead chrome shower heads. Four black marble stairs led to a huge matching hot tub that sat on its own pedestal overlooking the city, and black heated marble floors.

After the tour T-Roy prepared fillet mignon, baked potato, steamed asparagus and a Caesar salad. We ate on the outside balcony connected to his bedroom.

"This has to be the most tender piece of meat I've ever tasted." I said savoring the juicy steak.

"I try, he replied my grandmother taught me how to cook at an early age and ever since I've been hooked he added."

"So that exquisite kitchen isn't just for show?" I asked.

"Hell no I love to cook. I had my personal input on the whole design. If this music thing didn't work out my second choice would have been to own a restaurant." His passion was evident when he spoke about it.

"What would you name it? I asked.

"Oblivion," he simply stated.

"Why Oblivion?" I asked? "Because once you enter you forget where you have to go. My restaurant would have such a comfortable vibe you wouldn't want to leave."

"Oh I see." I said getting the picture. I tried to imagine his restaurant with a black and purple color scheme with a touch of fuchsia. The thought made me smile. "I think you should still open one up." I suggested.

"I've thought about it in the past but in all actuality I don't have the time D'Sire."

"Don't even go there you have nothing but time the first step has already been taken which is the thought process now all you have to do is put it on paper. You already have the means to make it happen so that shouldn't be problem. You're the only one that's hold you back." I retorted.

"You know D'Sire I've never thought about it in that way and I appreciate your insight. I guess the real reason for me not doing it is because it is such a challenge. When I sing its second nature so it's effortless but with the restaurant I'm not too sure."

"Well how would you know if you don't ever try?" I asked.

"Ok then how bout we make a deal?" He asked sparking my interest.

"Go ahead I'm listening." I said smiling.

"I'll put in the effort if you promise to help me out." He suggested.

"Ok you have yourself a deal. I got you on this one we could draw up a business plan within the next couple of weeks then go from there." I assured.

"Ok bet then its official. I can't believe I let you talk me into this."

"I talked you into what? Following your passion? Now you know these are the type of things I write about in the magazine. Does it really take you to have to meet me in person for you to take my advice?" I half joked back.

"You could say that." He teased. For the rest of the evening we laughed and talked about some of our expectations that we wanted from life. As well as our hopes and dreams. We drank several glasses of expensive champagne, fucked then passed out.

## CHAPTER 6

I awoke to the inviting smell of country hickory smoked slab bacon. I was too lazy to get out of the warm cushiony Tempur-Pedic bed that contoured my body. Dust particles danced in the steams of light that peeked in between the mirrored venetian blinds that separated the bedroom from the outside world. Through the cracked door I could faintly hear T-Roy voice through the disruption of pots and pans. It appeared to me as if he was having a heated discussion. I threw on one of his Armani Xchange white tees and made my way to the bathroom. In the mirrored incased cabinet over the sink I found a brand new toothbrush along with a tube of Listerine toothpaste. I pulled my hair to one side and held it so it wouldn't get in the minty path that streamed from my mouth. You would think that after all the dick I sucked my gag reflex would be trained by now but there is something about a toothbrush that always brings me to that point.

"I see you found everything ok." T-Roy said standing behind me. He lightly kissed the back of my neck causing the warm current that shot through my chakras make the tiny hairs on my body stand at attention. We made eye contact through our reflection in the mirror.

"We make a bomb ass couple." He said not breaking his stare. I have to admit we really did with my sun kissed skin next to his deep dark chocolate. T-Roy hoisted me on the counter. I wrapped my legs around his waist pulling him closer and deeply kissed him instantly causing his dick to stiffen against my thigh falling out of his boxers. Instantaneously I spread eagle allowing him to enter. T-Roy slowly stroked my pussy and sucked both my titties at the same time. He gently rolled my cinnamon colored nipples in between his tongue and teeth. I dug my bare heels in to the dip of his muscular back, forcing him deeper and deeper. T-Roy pulled out and lifted my legs on to his shoulders. I rested back on my forearms and watched him as he licked and sucked my juicy pussy. He entered me again this time with longer deeper strokes. He gazed into my eyes and memorized my soul. During that electrifying moment is when I climaxed. My pussy quivered on his thick hard dick. T-Roy let loose and I clenched putting it into a head lock and that's when he busts his first nut inside me. He rested between my legs for a brief moment heavily breathing. He took a cloth and soaped it up using warm water and washed the remnant of his seed from the opening of my lips. He then proceeded to wipe his own dick and nuts before putting the rag back on the sink. Why I just allowed this niggah to spit all up in me would have been the million-dollar question. And I did not have an answer even if my life depended on it. What I needed was a nice hot shower. There was a knock at the door followed by the chime of the bell. I peeped a slight smile on T-Roy's face as he left to answer. I was curious to who it could be but stayed behind due to my compromising attire. I wondered if it was that Beyonce' reject bitch from last night. Being nosey I couldn't make out the conversation just bits and pieces. One thing I was sure of was that it was a female's voice and T-Roy sounded very interested in what she had to say. I heard laughter followed by a pregnant pause. The door closed.

"D'Sire"

"Yes Troy." I sweetly answered.

"Come here for a minute I want to show you something." When I entered the living room that warm sensation flooded the inside of my chest again once I saw the display of gift boxes on the sofa.

"Well don't just stand there open them up all that's you ma." I stood stuck for a moment with my eyes wide.

"Oh my god thank you." I beamed holding both palms to my chest. I approached the 6 individually wrapped parcels like a shy child would Santa at the mall and looked back at T-Roy who was smiling at me. I opened the two smallest ones first. I pulled off the red, oversize bow to unleash the contents inside. It contained a pair of red Gucci stilettos. The next one was black Prada sling backs. I opened the long box next. Inside laid the special edition black and chrome Dolce & Gabbana thigh high boots with all the buckles and zippers that I told him about from the fashion show in Time Square that I covered last week. I took one out and hugged it close.

"How did you pull this off these aren't even out yet?" I asked.

"I know people who know people." Is all he said nodding his head, hinting me to open the rest. The next three contained a short black slant shoulder Gucci dress followed by three pair of Citizen for Humanity jeans and the last box contained an official pair of Christian Louboutin red bottom six inch heels. I stood up and jumped on T-Roy wrapping my legs around his waist.

"Thank you Troy." I said in between planting soft kisses on his lips. He carried me back to the bathroom and turned on the shower.

He fucked me so good from behind then washed me up. I dried off and got dressed and opted on wearing the dress. "You look beautiful bae."

"Thanks to you hooking me up." I replied.

"Nawww, you didn't need my help at all I'm talking about all that natural beauty you got going on."

"Oh thanks." I simply said.

"I have a few places to hit up today do you mind chillin wit your boy for a few more hours?"

"No problem I actually enjoy your company."

"Oh shit!" he exclaimed. I forgot about the breakfast I cooked for you. It's got to be cold now."

"It's okay we could just put your microwave to use."

"It aint going to taste the same." He said.

"I'm pretty sure it will still be good especially because you made it." I stood up and headed for the kitchen.

"What you doing?" T-Roy asked.

"Heating our food." I answered while fixing our plates.

"You are something else, so down to earth not stuck up like most woman I know."

"I'm not most women."

"I didn't mean it like that, I'm just saying your unique that's all."

"No offense taken. I just don't see the sense of wasting all this perfectly good food when there are so many starving people in the world ok."

"I respect that ma." He said holding his hands up palms facing me.

"I don't mean to sound so serious but my grandmother struggled to raise me and even though I live well now, I still can't forget what I've been through to get to where I am." I placed T-Roy's food on the table then put mine in the microwave next. I pulled out the black leather chair and sat at the table next to him. "Umm, see I told you it would still be good." I said after chewing the smoky bacon.

"Yea, yea, yea you were right but I want to get back to the conversation we were just having." A perplexed look came across my face.

"Uhh the conversation we were just having that you cut short once you mention your grandmother."

"I don't want to talk about it anymore." I said displaying some discomfort about the subject matter.

"As soon as you mentioned her the color literally drained from your face and your hands began to shake."

"I said I don't want to fuckin talk about it!"

"I'm sorry D'Sire I didn't mean to upset you."

"Let's just forget about it ok." I snapped. We ate in silence.

## CHAPTER 7

1995

and he would sand and paint in over for me in bright pinks and misty shades of purples. My father and mother were both absent in my life. A year after I was born. My dad caught a body and got sentenced to 25 years and soon after that my mother started smoking crack and shooting heroin. She was found dead in a motel room I'm not quite sure exactly what happened but one day I overheard my grandmother and my uncle talking about my mom saying that she owned some dealer money and threatened to set him up so he gave her some dope to bang but it had battery acid in it and her heart bust. I don't remember my mom and my grandmother said she's wasn't bringing me to no jail to see my father and asked him to sign his rights away and he did because he felt it was best so I've been in my grandmother house ever since I could remember. I even have my mother's old bedroom sometime I wonder how it would be if my mother was alive would uncle Jr. still want me or would he want my mom because she was prettier. I picked up the 8x10 picture of her that sat on my dresser. I held it up to my face and looked at us side by side in the mirror. We had the same green eyes and long hair except mine was curlier because my father was black but she had full breast and a small waist and big ass. I wonder if I will look like her one day I thought to myself and started to get jealous wondering if uncle Jr. Sucked her pussy like he do mine. I turned the picture face down on my dresser a part of me was glad she was dead. I took out a pair of no name jeans, panties, and an oversized blue Russell sweat shirt out of my dresser and laid them on my twin pink and white quilted bed spread. I washed up, got dressed, put my hair in a ponytail and headed for the bus stop. As usual Ant, Tyreek and Dayshawn were clowning on passersby's. They got on my nerves on the regular but were fun to be around. I just had to be sure to keep my distance just in case my uncle Jr rides by.

"What's up D? Tyreek was the first to acknowledge me.

"Heyy yall, what's good?" I said on approach.

"I know what's good" Dayshawn said while cracking a wicket grin. Ant busted out laughing. Tyreek elbowed Dayshawn which made Ant laugh even harder. For some reason I knew I was the butt of the joke.

"What the fuck are yall laughing at?" I said with attitude.

"Tyreek like you." Ant busted out. I crossed my arms in front of my chest and rolled my eyes at the trio.

"Y'all are so stupid I would never go out with either one of you because y'all act like little kids."

Ant and Dayshawn continued to laugh Dayshawn was rolling on the ground in his school clothes and Ant was slobbing everywhere choking. Tyreek just stood there and if looks could kill Ant and Dayshawn would have been two dead mutha fuckers. I was relieved to see the yellow school bus approaching in the distance. Its brakes screeched like a steam train when I come to a complete stop. I sucked my teeth and broke in between Tyreek and Ant not saying excuse me and waited for Mr. Miller our fat bus driver to open the doors. When he did I climbed up the stairs and avoided eye contact with him. I didn't like Mr. Miller he creeped me out by the way he licked his thin dry lips whenever I got on the bus. The kids were loud and obnoxious I just hated the whole school bus experience.

I made my way down the aisle toward my usual seat next to my best friend Dee Dee who was smiling as I approached. Dee Dee was gorgeous she had the lightest brown eyes I've ever seen her hair was straight and long to the middle of her back with a Chinese cut bang. She always rocked the latest fashion because she stayed in the malls boosting. She would always try to get me to go but I was too scared. I'm starting to have second thoughts because my gear is in a serious need for an upgrade. Dee Dee was two years older than me and developed she already fucked five boys. She still thinks I'm a virgin because I hold me and my uncle's secret close.

"Heyy girl why the mean face who fuckin wit you?" Dee Dee asked ready to throw blows.

"Nobody but them young dumb stupid acting boys Dayshawn and them at my bus stop talking about Tyreek like me."

"Ooo girl you better jump on that before I do. Tyreek is blazing with his curly black hair and light skin I wonder if he got a big dick."

"You is so crazy girl." I said but seriously contemplating. I never looked at Tyreek in that way but now to hear Dee Dee talk about him in that manor made me wonder too.

"D'Sire, you need to ask your grandmother if you could spend the night out at my house this weekend so I could teach you a few things and we could go to the mall and get you some stuff. It would be so much fun." she beamed.

"I'm not sure Dee Dee."

"Awww come on D'Sire, you don't never leave the house you act like an old lady. Everybody else go to the mall to have fun but you."

"It's not that I don't want to have fun Dee Dee, you know how my grandmother be buggin and shit all over protected." I lied truth was my uncle didn't want me to leave the house.

"Well at least try." She said.

"I will, today is only Monday I have a whole week to work on her." I assured.

"Ooooo, girl we gonna have so much fun. I can't wait and my mother be knocked out so we can sneak boys in the house and everything."

## CHAPTER 8

Convincing my grandmother wasn't the problem it was my uncle who gave me hell when I expressed my desire to spend the weekend with Dee Dee. We argued about it like a real couple would.

"You just want to go out so you could be fast around them no good niggahs out there he yelled."

"No I don't I just want to spend some time with Dee Dee and listen to music and have fun uncle Jr. That's all. I never get to do anything with my friends because I'm trapped in this basement fucking you all day." Baamm! Before I knew what hit me I was on the floor seeing stars. Blood began to flow from my nose.

"Oh you trapped now bitch, you be down here loving this dick. You be begging me to fuck yo little stank ass and now you want to walk around here all brand new talking about you want to go have fun with some so called best friend!" He towered over me and balls of dry spit spattered out his mouth as he spoke. The vein in his neck pump hard and his eyes were red, casting beams of hatred as he looked down upon me. "Now go clean yo ass up and come back here and show uncle Jr. how much you love this dick D'Sire." He said while unbuckling his jeans. He took his swollen member out and began to stroke it.

I scraped myself off the floor and did as I was told I tilted my head back and tasted blood as it trickled down the back of my throat. I felt for my wash cloth and wet it with cold water then placed it on my throbbing nose. Salty tears left trails as they flowed down the path on my face and off my chin. I applied pressure finally stopped the bleeding but the swelling was still present. I looked at my reflection in the mirror I felt so ugly and unloved. I slid down the wall and my body spasmed from uncontrollable sobbing. That was just one of the many explosive episodes I went through with my uncle anytime I voiced myself. He would beat the shit out of me, break me down then lift me back up fucking me really good. He would look me in my eyes while on top and tell me how much he loved and needed me, making me forget about the whole ugly episode and once again I felt validated.

"So what she say?" Dee Dee asked before I had the chance to take my seat.

"I still didn't talk to her yet." I lied looking straight ahead.

"Wait a minute what the fuck happened to your face?" I jerked away.

"I was behind my door and my grandmother came barging in my room like always without knocking and the door damn there took my nose off." Dee Dee did not seem convinced.

"So what do you have planned for us this weekend?" I asked changing the subject.

"I thought you said you didn't talk to her yet." She asked with a raised arched eyebrow.

"I didn't, that don't mean shit I'm still coming no matter what she says."

"That's what I'm talking about!" She exclaimed giving me dap, suddenly forgetting about my bruised nose.

"Girrl we gonna have so much fun I can't wait oh my god do you think I should tell Tyreek to come through? We could meet him at the mall. No neva mind, he might fuck up our flow. I could call Tone and he can come get us smoked out." She went on without taking a breath. I couldn't help but to laugh at her because she was so animated and her eyes were all big. Somehow some way I had to make a way out of no way and I had no idea how. Behind my smile I hid my true emotions which reeked of fear.

As soon as we pulled up to Wilber Cross Middle School Dee Dee put her prepaid cell phone on silent then took out a black Mac compact from her brown monogrammed Coach bag along with a Mac clear lip gloss and quickly applied it to her full luscious lips. "I can't wait till this weekend girl Ima make you up." She cooed.

Once in school we parted our separate ways. I had a hard time concentrating on my test. Because I was so consumed with what I would tell my uncle to get out of the house and afraid of the consequence once he found out I've lied to him. My heart began to jump hurdles in my chest and my throat clenched tight as the class room began to close in on me. Rain drop size sweat bead leaped out of my pours onto the paper on the desk drowning out my penciled answers. I felt a wetness in my panties I raised my shaky hand to get Mrs. Richards my math teacher's attention.

"Yes D'Sire."

"May I be excused I need to go to the bathroom." Mrs. Richards put her papers down and walked over to my desk. She took off her glasses and a look of concern washed over her face as she led me to the hallway out of ear shot of the class.

"D'Sire are you ok? Where did you get those bruises from?"

"Mrs. Richards, I really don't feel well."

"Ok D'Sire, you may go to the bathroom then you need to go to the nurse's office." She said before putting her glasses back on. I was thankful to have the bathroom to myself. I pushed the silver pump with my palm then caught the water with my other hand and splashed it on my face. It felt nice and cool against my clammy skin. Next I entered the stall. The swing back door squeaked when I pushed it open and I locked it behind me. I slowly unbuttoned my jeans and slid my panties down. My legs felt awkward like they didn't match my body. A picture of my uncle flashed before me causing me to lose my balance and I hit my head against the stall's wall. The image of my uncle fucking a very little girl flooded my mind I stood in my body and watched as if I was peeking in the window of a stranger's house. Blood and fecal matter was smeared all over the sheets and wall. I saw him carry her to the bathroom and turn on the light.

He ran a tub of water and put her in it and splashed water on her face as he called her name, "D'Sire oh my god, D'Sire wake up!" Then I saw my grandmother screaming at my uncle and hitting him with tight but weak fists.

"Edwin what the fuck did you do to my baby?"

"No, no that wasn't me!" I screamed holding my head with both my hands.

"D'Sire please open the door." It was Mrs. Orlando the schools nurse with my teacher. I had no idea how long they been standing there.

"I'm coming out now." I stammered, I hurried to pull up my panties afraid of exposing my secret and unlatched the door that separated us. I sheepishly emerged from the stall with my head down and walked between them back to the sink.

"Oh I see the problem Mrs. Richards. D'Sire we need to call your grandmother." Mrs. Orlando spoke.

"No please don't he didn't do it I swear please don't call her." I pleaded.

"Do what D'Sire? Don't worry it's alright every girl about your age goes through it." She said trying to assure me.

"They do?" I asked quite surprised.

"Yes it's one of the stages that your body goes through when it wants to change."

"Change? I don't understand what you're saying Mrs. Orlando." I was really scarred now.

"D'Sire honey you just had your first menstrual period." She said smiling.

"You'll be fine. Mrs. Richards I'll take it from here. I'm going to bring D'Sire to my office and call her grandmother to come pick her up. Thank you for your help." She graciously said then we walked to her office.

## CHAPTER 9

2010

"D'Sire would you come to my office please?" Monica my boss asked as I walked to my desk.

"Sure Monica I'll be right there." I said putting my blue checkered leather Louis Vuitton briefcase in its respective spot. In my mind curious thoughts fought over what she wanted. I lightly tapped on the door.

"Come in D'Sire." I turned the cold brass knob and the heavy solid oak door creaked open allowing me access to the luxurious spacious quarters. It had a Feng shui type of vibe to it. The walls were a burnt red with huge gold framed Japanese art. There was a beautifully kept live Bonsai Tree in a corner opposite to her clear desk that appeared to float above a red, black and gold imported rug. She sat in a high back plush leather chair in front of a huge window that displayed a full sky view of the Hartford CT State capitol giving her a presidential aura.

"What's good Monica?" I asked trying to feel out her mood.

"This is." She simply said tossing The New York Post on her desk. On the front page was a picture of T-Roy and I walking out of the motel room. The headline read R&B sensation T-Roy gets cozy with mystery girl.

"Go ahead open it there's more." She pointed. I could not believe what I saw. There was a full page spread about us with pictures from the mall, Toads place and in front of his sky rise. I was glad they left out my condo.

"Oh my God! I exclaimed and dropped the paper "Monica I can explain." I started before she cut me off.

"Girl no need to get all nervous now I'm just surprise that I had to find out this way. I thought we were closer than that.

"Once people find out who you are this could mean big time business for the magazine." She said beaming at me from her desk. "By the way you looked gorgeous in those leather pants girl." She gave me a wink with a smile. I did not know what to make out what I just saw but I had a feeling that things were about to change around here. I received a phone call from T-Roy.

"Did you see it?" He asked.

"Yes how did they know?" I wanted to know.

"That's the thing these people are thorough with they shit. They will do anything to get a story." He answered.

"What you doing?" He asked.

"I just left out my boss's office she showed me the article."

"Wow, news travels fast."

"I know but it's expected because we have access to all magazine and papers 24 hours a day.

As soon as it leaves the press they come straight to her desk. There was no way this would have gotten pass her."

"Was she mad?" He asked.

"No, actually she seemed ok with it all she was just disappointed because I didn't tell her first but I don't feel as though I am obligated to broadcast my personal business to her no matter how close we are."

"I feel you on that. I miss your sexy ass." That made me smile I could just imagine his dick getting hard.

"Then do something about it."

"What time do you get off?" He asked.

"Round six, then I'm heading home to play catch up with an overdue assignment."

"Can I slide through for a minute?" He asked.

"Yea, as long as you leave your camera crew behind with their slick asses."

"I'll try ok TTYL bout to go in the booth." My phone alerted me that a text came through. Smile. That T-Roy put on my face disappeared once I read the contents.

It said, "Bitch you better watch your back I'm coming for your head." The number was anonymous. I thought about texting T-Roy but remembered that he was in the booth so I decided to save it and show him later. I reset my phone to reject all future anonymous calls and texts. Whoever it was, was a straight up fucking coward for hiding behind the protection of their cell phone, and that shit burnt me up inside.

The person could have had the wrong number though but I wasn't going to sleep on the situation either and wait for somebody to run up on me. So I made the conscious decision to take my bitch out from top of the closet when I got home. It's been a while since I used her but if needed we, can reacquaint really quick. I don't have a problem with poppin a niggah.

Angel our fashion columnist slid her chair to my cubicle in a nosey attempt to find out what Monica and I talked about pretending to show me all the post errors the fashion editor intern missed. Totally uninterested in what she had to say I simply tuned her out. She had all the latest dirt on everybody lives I wasn't giving her the satisfaction of gaining access into mine until Saul aka Sasha Fierce, her photographer sashayed his bubble butt over our way.

"D'Sire you little hoe when was you going to tell us about the lil rendezvous with your fine ass boy toy T-Roy?" He said with his manicured hand on his hip.

"What? Who? T-Roy the singer T-Roy or T-Roy from the hood T-Roy ooo girl you have to tell us we want all the details." Angel squealed.

"Sasha got the paper why don't you just read what it says." I dryly stated clearly aggravated.

"No girl we rather hear it straight from the horse's mouth." Sasha said in Z formation.

"I can't believe y'all two bitches are double teaming me." I said with a shocked expression. Even though they were nosey as hell we were all pretty close. Ever since I began working for the magazine about a year ago these two along with my boss became my make believe family the only thing is now that my business is on blast, this is their first true glance into my private life because I simply refuse to talk about it so I could see why it was such a big deal to them especially with T-Roy being a celebrity so I spoon fed them enough to keep them off my back for now. I bent the story a little bit about how we met. I told them that I tracked him down to write an article on his new album that just dropped and we went out a few times.

"Nothing big." I said "You know how the paper over exaggerates the truth." I added for emphases.

"I knew you were an undercover slut but guess what? So am I, that's why we make the perfect team. So when are we going to meet Mr. T-Roy?" He inquired.

"Well I wasn't thinking…" I said before getting cut off.

"Now now no need to be selfish with the goods lil miss D'Sire, I think it's time that you host a dinner party. It's a shame that we all been working together for over a year now and none of us ever been to your crib". He did have a point there I guess It was time to allow them a small peek in to my world. All these two ever do is gossip all day. Really what harm could they do? I thought to myself.

"Well let me see how T-Roy feels about it and I promise to get back at y'all." I said.

"Ok bitch don't make me hunt yo ass down." Sasha said trying to sound ghetto. His comment made me laugh.

"Yea ok." I said nearly in stitches. That day neither one of us hardly got any work done. I was so backed up I could of killed both Angel and Sasha. It was all worth it though because I was beginning to feel as though my life finally had some sense of normalcy.

## CHAPTER 10

After work I drove to a local market to purchase a few items. Amongst them were fresh jumbo shrimp, 2 dozen cherry stone clams and two Porter House steaks for the grill. In the same shopping plaza there was also a package store so I copped a bottle of Perrier Joue't white wine which tasted fabulous with grilled sea food. I heard my viper alarm sounding. Upon approaching my car, I noticed a long key type scratch on the driver side door of my Benz and there were five big jagged letters that spelled bitch.

What the fuck I hastily pushed the cart out of the way to get a better examination of the damage. I dialed the police and my insurance company to give them a report and drove home wondering who in the hell would do this to me because it was no random act. First the text earlier now this shit. One thing was for sure some body was clearly out to get me and for them to vandalize my car in a full parking lot in broad day light meant they were brazen enough to take risks which indicated to me that this person's actions were fueled by emotions. Aware of my surroundings I made sure not to take the usual route home. I felt as if I was being watched but no same car followed me. Once inside the safety of my condo I felt somewhat relieved. I took off my Gucci pumps and placed my brief case on the sofa then walked to my bedroom's closet and the automatic track light came on once I opened the door. Amongst the hundreds of boxes of shoes lay my 9mm caliber glock off safety and loaded. I picked up the cold black steel closed my eyes, then kissed her before placing it in the night stand beside my bed.

My cell phone rang it was the insurance company, "Hello hi may I speak with Ms. D'Sire Gomez?"

"This is she."

"Hello Ms Gomez I just wanted to let you know that we handled everything for you and at your earliest convenience we would like to send one of our agents out to assess the damage." The friendly operator said.

"Is tomorrow good?" I asked.

"Sure we could have someone out their first thing in the morning. Would you need a ride to the rental place?"

"I'm not sure I'll have to get back at you with that my boyfriend might bring me." I caught myself say.

"Ok either way no problem. Also do you have a place in mind to tow it to?"

"Yes I have my own private mechanic and I've already left a message for him so he should be getting in touch with me soon."

"Okay Ms. Gomez is 9:30 am ok with you?"

"That's fine I really appreciate your prompt services in this manner." I genuinely said.

"Oh it's no problem." She assured. We said our good byes and disconnected. I dialed T-Roy next.

"Heyy baby what's good?"

"T-Roy I need to talk to you." There was a pause.

"Are you aight D'Sire?" He sounded real concerned.

"Well yea sort of." I solemnly stated.

"I was just about to call you to let you know that I was on my way." Now he sounded nervous.

"Well it could wait until you get here and it's not an emergency so don't go killing yourself or anybody to else speeding." I said to lighten things up.

"Ok baby I'll be there in about an hour or so depending on traffic."

"Ok I'll be here hope you like seafood." I threw in before disconnecting. I picked up the remote and pointed it at my stereo and the cd changer I switched it from Beyonce's B-day to Young Money's CD then remembered that I left the groceries in the car so I had to go all the way downstairs to the parking lot. I threw on a pair of pink and black Air Maxes, grabbed my keys and headed out the door. I disabled my alarm and retrieved the bags from the trunk of my car. From peripheral vision outside the gate of my condo I peeped an all-black Range Rover with the blackest tints I've ever seen. It sat on chrome Denali rims. A chill ran first up then down my body. I stood frozen. The passenger automatic window rolled down and an attractive light skin woman with grey eyes of steel and long straight jet black hair called out.

"Excuse me I am lost could you please tell me where 95 South is?"

"Sure take a left down Old Town Rd and around the bin then go under the bridge and make another left and you will see it." I gladly gave her the directions.

"Thank you." She sweetly said and pulled off. She had New York plates but I didn't think much of it so I locked my trunk and headed back up to my place to start the grill. I looked amongst my many pots and dishes until I found my deep nonstick baking pan, strainer and two cutting boards. I carefully washed all the meat paying extra attention to the steak making sure to tenderize and season to perfection next I covered them and placed them in the fridge. I used my scrubber to washer the dirt off of the closed clam shells and placed them into the strainer in the sink. I prepared an avocado and tomato salad with red onion, fresh cracked black pepper and feta cheese, tossed it up and put it in the fridge next to the steak.

I washed my hands and switched CD's to Lil Wayne's Carter III. Then started my gas grill on the patio and put the heat to the lowest settings. I welcomed the smell of the salty air and my dynamic view of the sea. This patio has been my sanctuary my refuge whenever I needed help tapping into my creative source.

I come here to mediate and suddenly my mind flows with all the brightest ideas of when my problems seem too big to handle. I seem to find all the solutions right here. Sometimes at night I sit out here and allow the moon to hypnotize me and I watch the beautiful blue black sky for hours. I figured I still had some time so I decided to take my shower and freshen up before T-Roy got here. I knew I would need another one later but I just needed to wash away the stress of the day off my body and shave. I peeled out my clothes and threw them in the hamper. Once in the shower I allowed the steam to penetrate my pours and exfoliated with a super body scrub I personally made in kiwi strawberry. Once I rinsed off I soaped up my body with an all-natural matching soap to the body scrub and shaved my pussy paying extra attention to the delicate lips. Next my legs and underarms. I washed up three more times and was finished. I grabbed my big fluffy Michael Kors white bath towel and wrapped it around my smooth soft scented body.

The fruity smell of the bathroom permeated the whole house once I opened the door. I laid across my bed and air dried, what I loved the most about my body scrubs was that I never had to lotion after using them and the smell was to die for. I decided to put on pink and white Juicy Couture and Juicy pink flip flops that showed off my pretty manicured toes. I opened up my bedroom window then headed for the kitchen. The flashing red light on my cell phone stopped me in my tracks so I scrolled through to see what calls and or texts I missed. Two from Sasha Fierce.

"Let me call this bitch back." I said out loud. The phone didn't get to ring twice before Sasha's voice blurred through.

"Bitch what are you doing?"

"Nothing just got out the shower. What's good?"

"Oh I just wanted to see if you talked to T-Roy yet that's all."

"Didn't I tell you that I would get back at you after I talk to him?"

"Trick listen you said that over five hours ago and I know you talked to him since then." My line beeped it was T-Roy.

"Sasha I promise I got you on this ima holla at your later." He tried to protest but I clicked him off connecting my call to T-Roy.

"Hey baby I'm outside the gate."

"Ok I'm about to buzz you in." I ran to my room to double check that I secured my ratchet then applied a thin coat of Mac lip gloss across my lips.

My intercom beeped and T-Roy's image filled the security screen so I buzzed him in. A few moments later he appeared at my door.

"Hi Troy." I said before giving him a closed lip kiss. He palmed my ass and closed the door behind him. He walked to the patio.

"Oh word your bout to grill it up for a niggah?" He said with a sexy smile.

"Yea a lil sumtin." I said. He lifted the top.

"Where the food at ma? I'm hungry like a hostage" He joked.

"Still marinating in the fridge it should be bout ready by now." I said making my way to the kitchen to check.

"Yea it is." I poked the tender meat with a long grilling fork.

"What you got there?" T-Roy asked entering the kitchen.

"Two Porter House steaks some clams and shrimp oh and a Greek salad." I added.

"That's what's up bae." T-Roy said clasping his palms together. "So what you have to tell me?" He asked changing the subject. I picked up my phone and showed him the text then the pictures of my car. "Yo, who the fuck would do some shit like this to you?" He asked clearly heated. I didn't even notice nothing wrong with your car when I pulled up."

"That's because you have to be up on it to see because of the color." I explained while adding my special homemade steak rub on the meat. I then walked back to the patio and placed them both on the hot grill that awaited and washed my hands. We took our places on the couch.

"So when are you getting your car fixed?"

"Tomorrow they are going to come pick it up." I answered. Is there anything I could do? T-Roy asked.

"No I'm good I just need to get a rental for the week that's all. My insurance company said they would handle everything. I just wish I knew who did this and wonder if they know where I live. It just creeps me out that somebody is watching me so close."

"I can stay with you for a few days, that's if you don't mind."

"No, I don't mind only if you want though."

"I'll stay tonight then tomorrow we could go pick up your rental and after I'll head up top to pick up some things from my crib. You going to work tomorrow?"

"No Ima take the day off to run some errands."

"Ok then as soon as we get the rental I'll handle my B.I. then I'll slide back through."

"Yea that sounds like a plan." I said beaming on the inside. After the steaks cooked thoroughly I spread olive oil on the foil then placed the jumbo shrimp and cherry stones on the grill. When the clams began to open I splashed a lemon butter sauce that I made on them. Everything was done so I shut the grill off and prepared our plates. I took the wine out of the fridge, opened it then placed it in a metal bucket full of ice on the table.

The sun began to set the sky contrasted with a rich color scheme of fuchsia, orange and indigo. We ate our meals and when darkness fell I lit two patio Tiki torches which casted a soft light giving off a relaxing ambience.

## CHAPTER 11

It's been about three weeks since the last time I saw T-Roy and even though we talked on the phone every day. I was finding myself missing his presence I couldn't help but feel gratified when he stayed with me for a few days after the incident with my car traveling to and from the city to work in the studio with another well know artist, Isis who collaborated on a few songs with him. When I wasn't working he would bring me with him and it felt so good to have him to myself every night and I've gotten quite use to waking up to hot sex with him on a platter in the morning. On the last day I seized the opportunity to bring up the subject of the possibility of me throwing my first dinner party and how my colleagues were dying to meet him. To my surprise he agreed to attend without hesitation. I also asked him to bring a few heads to entertain the ladies. I glanced at my desk calendar. The date was Thursday August 5th my party was only nine days away to be exact and I was feeling upbeat in spirit eagerly anticipating the outcome. The last time, I had a party was when I was six years old and my grandmother just suddenly stop giving them. They weren't much fun anyways nobody was ever invited just me her and my uncle. I never knew any better though I thought that was how every kid celebrated until I started school and all the other kids would talk about their birthdays or sometimes mother and fathers would come to the class with cupcakes and surprise them and only then did I realized even at such a young age that me being different was an understatement.

I felt a surge of negative energy slither up my spine and coil into the pit of my stomach. I unconsciously physically shook the bad memory out of my head. Thankfully the gesture went undetected I held certification in masking my true feelings while in the company of others. I continued throughout the workday trying my best to avoid the subject matter but Sasha made it very hard for me with this endless questioning about the venue and insisted on helping me put it all together. I tried to decline his advances but he was relentless.

"D'Sire girl you just have to let me help you I know just the right place we can go to get everything you need for this party." He said with much enthusiasm.

"Sasha I do appreciate the gesture but I have the situation under control this isn't my first diner party." I lied trying to keep my voice indifferent.

"Move over bitch let me just show you something really quick." He said pushing my swivel chair with me in it to the side. My protests went unanswered. Sasha minimized the computer screen with my work. His manicured fingers struck the keys with vigorous speed.

"Voila." He chimed popping his lips. Using one leg I scooted my chair back in front of the screen. Party Nation the one stop party shop. Everything you need to plan that special event under one roof.

"Thanks Sash." I wrote the web address and quickly closed the screen before he could respond. "I have a ton of work that I need to finish up if I don't have no job then I can't have no party right?"

"Ok bitch Ima let you off the hook for now cause lord only knows if you lose your job I don't do the loan thing." He said as if I would ask him anyway. Sasha sashayed towards Angel's desk and immediately began engaging in the latest gossip with her. A few hours passed and I was putting on the last finishing touch of my article on soul searching through hip hop and suddenly I became inspired to do a lil soul searching of my own. I saved my work and emailed it to Monica then began typing. The challenges that call us forth are driving us to personal transformation. We are more than our limited thoughts and physical selves. When we begin to accept this then our conscious expands giving ourselves a much broader sense of identity. This is silly. I thought to myself and pushed the delete button. Then I retyped what I deleted and decided to save it. I turned off my computer and gathered my things. The office was nearly empty Sasha and Angel both ran out talking about meeting up at the lounge and invited me but as always I declined using work as my excuse. I glanced at my watch it read 5:15 p.m.

"Time to go." I said out loud and left the office into the beautiful summer warm breezy rest of the day that awaited me. After my 45-minute commute from work I decided to detour and stop at my favorite bistro down town New Haven to grab a bite to eat because I had no intention on cooking. My plans involved researching that website that Sasha gave me earlier and drinking the rest of the wine I had stashed in the back of my fridge. I walked into the dimly lit restaurant and was greeted by a very attractive woman of Asian descent who looked to be in her mid-twenties. She had beautiful flawless porcelain doll skin full naturally red lips and her jet black straight hair, had a healthy sheen to it like a horse's mane.

"Hello welcome to Malcolm's." she said flashing dazzling perfect white teeth.

"Would you prefer a seat in main dining or outside on the terrace?" She asked. My pussy pulsed.

I was attracted to her "Um outside please."

"Right this way." She picked up a menu.

"Will someone be joining you?" She smiled and asked.

"No I'm by myself today." She seated me at a table next to a couple whom to me seemed to be deeply in love. The man held both of the woman's hands in his and she seemed captivated by whatever he was saying. Neither one of them glanced my way. The hostess placed the faux black leather menu that read Malcolm's in shimmering elegant gold script in front of me when I sat down. I always took my time reading the menu although I practically knew it by heart. A nice looking tan Caucasian waiter with short spiked hair approached my table smiling.

"Hi my name is Matt I will be serving you this evening. May I offer you something to drink?" He politely asked while placing a tall glass in front of me. He poured water into it from a clear glass pitcher.

"Yes, I would like a glass of white wine please." I answered returning a smile.

"Would you like to order now or would you like a moment to decide?" He asked.

"A few more minutes please." I answered.

"Ok I'll be back to take your order." He said and strolled to the next table behind me. I took advantage of the free moment and decided to hit the lady's room to freshen up. On my way back to the table a woman abruptly stopped in front of me and I accidently ran into her causing her to spill her drink all over herself.

"Oh my god I am so sorry."

I said trying to help. "No need to apologize it was actually my fault for stopping so suddenly but I forgot my…" She stopped mid-sentence when our eyes met.

"Don't I know you from somewhere?" She changed up.

"I don't think so although you do look familiar." I said with a perplexed look.

"Wait a minute I remember now you're the one who gave me directions to the highway a few weeks ago." She said smiling. I had to think back. Then it hit me.

"Oh yea I do remember now how could I forget; you have the most unique set of grey eyes I've ever saw." I complimented.

"Miss could we have some club soda please?" I asked the hostess. "Girl is that Channel? I hope it's not ruined." I said eyeing her cream dress.

"Nothing a little dry cleaning can't handle." She assured. The hostess brought the club soda over and handled me a white linen napkin.

"Let's go into the bathroom where there's more light." I suggested. I dipped the napkin in the glass and blotted the stain out to the best of my ability.

"Girl I do appreciate your help." She said with sincerity.

"No problem it's the least I can do for practically running you over." I lightly joked.

"Also let me buy you another drink." I added.

"You really don't have to." She tried to decline.

"I know I don't but I insist. What table are you at? I'll have the waiter bring it right to you." I said.

"Well actually I was sitting over there at the bar waiting for somebody but he never showed so I was about to head on out."

"I'm outside on the terrace your more than welcomed to join me if you like."

"Are you sure I don't want to impose on you and your company."

"Girl you're not I'm actually having dinner by myself and I could use the company." I assured.

"Oh and by the way my name is D'Sire." I said extending my hand.

"Nice to meet you D'Sire my name is Jazzlyn." She shook my hand and we exited the bathroom. I led the way to my table while she followed. The couple from earlier were still at their table enjoying each other this time I spotted huge marquee diamond engagement ring on her left hand. They were embraced in a kiss. How beautiful he must have proposed to her I thought to myself.

"Have a seat Jazzlyn." I gestured towards the empty chair we both sat at the same time.

"D'Sire, you can call me Jazz for short."

"Ok Jazz are you hungry?"

"Actually I am starving." She said rubbing her flat stomach. The waiter came to our table.

"I thought you left. I see you have company now. Would you like another menu?" He asked.

"No thanks she can have mine I already know what I want." I answered. He took a small spiraled tablet out of the front pocket of his black slacks. I ordered grilled salmon with rice pilaf and a house salad.

"You know what D'Sire that sounds good I think I'll have the same."

"What kind of dressing would you ladies like?" He asked.

"Balsamic." We said in unison. We looked at each other and laughed.

"Would you still like that glass of white wine?" He asked looking at me.

"Sure." I answered.

"And what can I get for you?"

"I would like Grey goose and cranberry juice please." Jazzlyn said

"Ok ladies I will be right back with your beverages." He came back quickly with three glasses. He placed our drinks on the table in front of us and our drinks on the table in front of us and poured water in the empty glass and replenished mine. The couple beside us was gathering their things to leave. "Congratulations." I called out to them. They thanked me and smiled before disappearing into the crowd inside. The waiter was back with our salads and fresh bake bread sticks with two small white ceramic containers that held melted garlic butter sauce for dipping.

"Oh my god this bread is to die for." Jazzlyn said closing her eyes to savor.

"Girl you don't know? Malcolm's has the best food in town." I said.

"So Jazz where are you from?" I asked. She hesitated before answering.

"I'm from Paramus New Jersey."

"Oh I'm out there at least three times a month they have some exclusive shit." I said.

"So I was right it is a Channel piece correct?" I said with assumption.

"As a matter of fact it is your pretty good." She said.

"Girl I have an eye for high end fashion I can spot authenticity a mile away." I added with confidence.

"So what brings you to Connecticut?" I continued to probe.

"I was actually meeting a friend of mine here then he was supposed to take me apartment hunting tomorrow I was going to stay at a hotel tonight." She said with a look of concern.

"Did you check your phone maybe he called or something?" I asked. She reached in her purse. "Oh my god I feel so stupid. My phone was on silent and he called several times. I better call him back." Jazzlyn excused herself from the table and returned several minutes later.

"Is everything ok?" I asked.

"Yea, he said he tried to call me earlier to cancel because he had to do an emergency surgery. He's a Dr at Yale Hospital." she said smiling.

"He was a little worried but all is forgiven. I told him I was here having dinner with you and that I was still staying. He said that he will be in surgery for at least eight more hours and couldn't promise to meet me tomorrow." She added.

"A Dr's job is demanding." I told her.

"Well tomorrow is my day off maybe I can show you around." I suggested.

"No D'Sire can't you've been nice enough I'm pretty sure you got better things to do on your day off than show me around town." She said.

"Yea I probably do. I joked, but no seriously all I'm doing tomorrow is picking up a few things for my dinner party and for the rest of the day I'm free honestly I don't mind." Our food arrived.

"This food looks delicious." She said.

"It does but I can guarantee it tastes even better." I said preparing to take a bite. Jazzlyn blew on her food to cool it down first then placed a fork full of the flakey fish into her mouth.

"Ummm D'Sire this has to be the best fish I've ever tasted. I would do just about anything to know the secret to the marinade that they use." She said.

"Me too." I agreed we ate the rest of our meals and ordered one more drink.

"What hotel are you crashing at tonight?" I asked

"I made reservations at the Courtyard Marriott on Whalley Ave."

"Oh I know exactly where that's at its not too far from here. Do you know the way?" I asked.

"Yea, I have it programmed on the GPS from my phone." She said. The waiter returned to our table.

"Would you two ladies be having desert this evening?"

"Oh no I'm stuffed." I said.

"None for me either." Jazzlyn said.

"May I please just have the bill?" I asked and noticed Jazzlyn reach into her purse. I stopped her.

"I got this." And handed him my American Express. He returned with the receipt and I wrote down his tip. A huge grin spread across his lips.

"Thank you miss thank you so much!" He exclaimed as if I made his day.

"Your quite welcome thank you for your impeccable services." I said. He flashed one more smile then proceeded to wait a new set of patrons who just entered his station. Jazzlyn and I sat for several more minutes and conversed about our next day plans.

"D'Sire, I am so grateful for you thank you I really had a nice time this evening." We exchanged cell phone numbers.

"I had a good time with you too. I'll come scoop you around noon ok. Oh and make sure to go to a store and pick up a New Haven Register and get a head start by calling a few places in the morning k."

"Ok will do. I'll see you tomorrow then." She said and we parted ways. I finally made it home around 8:30 p.m. a little bit later than expected. It was all good though because it was nice to chill with someone outside of work. I relieved my feet from confines of my heels and headed straight for my fuchsia wireless I Mac laptop and punched in the web address. Within seconds the site was up. I tripped over my briefcase running to the fridge to claim my bottle of wine.

"Fuck!" I grabbed the bottle and a glass then limped back to the living room. I poured a full glass and sipped while viewing the site. Sasha was right this definitely was the place I needed to order the stuff for my party from. The nearest location was in Hamden. I wrote the address and phone number down and decided to pay them a visit tomorrow as well. I finished the last of the wine and dosed off right there on the couch I was tipsy as hell.

## CHAPTER 12

1998

"Come on D'Sire get in." I looked around nervous as hell.

"Girl get yo scary ass in the car. We going shopping." Dee Dee said.

"Hey D'Sire." Dee Dee's boyfriend Trent said as I hopped into the back seat of his black 1999 Mercedes E class.

"Hi Trent". I dryly said rolling my eyes. On more than one occasion he made advances towards me. I remember one in particular when I was getting out of his car. His hand palmed my ass. Dee Dee was oblivious though and I did not dare tell her because she was madly in love with him. She met him the first week she started the ninth grade he was a senior and one of the cutest boys in her high school He had curly jet black hair, olive toned skin and chinky eyes. Dee Dee's popularity skyrocketed literally overnight. Me on the other hand was still in middle school going on the 8th grade and overly developed for my age. My hips were wider than my waist and my titties looked like swollen pears. I was very mature and people often mistaken me to be 18years or older.

"D'Sire, I was just telling Trent how he needs to hook you up with one of his boys.

I know you tired of being the third wheel in this relationship." She said before sparking a blunt. She took two tokes then passed it to me. I inhaled the potent smoke into my lungs. By the smell and taste of it I recognized it as Hydro. After the second toke I began to feel its intoxication effect. We passed it back and forth. Trent didn't smoke because he always talked about staying on point incase niggahs roll up and shit. We drove around for a little smoking Trent stayed chirping on his Nextel speaking in code something about needing two tires because he had a flat. He kept his eye on me through the rearview during his conversation I felt uncomfortable. We pulled up to the mall. I watched as he gave Dee Dee an undisclosed amount of bills. Dee Dee wrapped her arms around his neck and kissed him deep and slow on the lips "Thank you baby." She squealed.

"Damm bitch I didn't know Trent was hittin you off like that." I said clearly in shock.

"Yea girl that's my reward for all the head I give him." She bragged "He tells me that I give the best top and how no other woman pussy is as good as mine." She added. I smiled inward knowing that Trent lied to her because my uncle tells me the same thing except he doesn't give me money as a reward. He tells me he loves me instead. She never mentioned Trent ever telling her though. So I felt a sense of victory.

"Girl I got Trent open he doesn't know I be boosting all this expensive shit I be wearing." She said.

"He doesn't?" I asked surprised.

"Hell no and I don't plan on ever telling him either girl I be stacking my paper. I'm trying to buy me something chunky and

I need my own crib ya heard." She said stuffing the bills in her black and grey Dooney & Burke drawstring book bag. We entered Macy's.

"Watch this." She said and grabbed an arm full of Guess jeans and shirts off the rack then walked to the counter. "Ma'am, may I please have a bag mine ripped." She said holding up a torn Macy's bag.

"Sure here you go." The older Caucasian sales woman said smiling.

"Thank you." Dee Dee said, and walked away hitting up various racks undetected. I couldn't believe how easy this shit was. We waited for a crowd of people to exit the store and blended in. The alarm went off and my heart froze. Dee Dee yanked me and we entered the next store, Nordstrom's. Dee Dee handed me the Macy's bag full of stolen merchandise and played the whole scenario over again. Between the two stores she had to have over five grand worth of clothes. We stayed in the mall for about two hours shopping then called Trent to come get us. He was there in about 10 minutes.

"Damn bae you put a dent in them stores huh." He said grabbing several bags out of our hands smiling.

"Yall hungry?" He asked.

"Yea all that shopping got me famine?" Dee Dee said.

"Me too." I truthfully added. We wound up going to the Olive Garden in Hamden. The food was good and I was feeling saucy from the two Heinekens I drank. Dee Dee excused herself from the table.

"Yo D'Sire, you know you sexy as hell right? When you gonna let me hit that? I'll give you whatever you want."

"Trent, you aint nothing but a no good dirty dog. You better leave me the fuck alone before I tell Dee Dee." I said with my eyebrows narrowed.

"Go head she aint gonna believe you." He said mockingly.

"What eva Trent." Dee Dee sat down all smiles.

"What's wrong D'Sire aint you having a good time?"

"Yea, I am I'm just a little tired that's all." I said not looking at her.

"That's because you need to get out more, Trent call that niggah Jamal and hook D'Sire up we can rent a room and get nice. D'Sire you remember Jamal right?"

"Yea the blazin one hook it up Trent." I said trying to sound up beat. Trent squinted his eyes at me on the low.

"Aight I'll let you know what he says let's get going I got some business to handle." Trent dropped Dee Dee and me off at her house. Once inside she divided the clothes up amongst the two of us. She handed me four Stop –n- Shop bags.

"Here put your stuff in these." I gave her a perplexed look.

"Duhhh how else would you explain to your grandmother all this new shit? Just tell her that I was cleaning out my closet and I gave it all to you." She said ripping tags off.

"And here, you need a new book bag." She tossed me her Dooney & Burke.

"Thank you." I smiled. Up until now I've never owned one piece of name brand clothing. I was full of gratitude.

"D'Sire you're not a little girl any more it's time for you to step your game up and get money. You got to come out of that shy virgin shit, girl you're sitting on a goldmine you can have any niggah you want. All you have to do is fuck him really good and he will come out his pockets deep for you just like Trent does for me. I know for a fact that Jamal's money is long and I heard through the grape vine that he got a big dick." She said with emphasis.

"Wait don't he got a baby by Tasha?" I asked.

"Girl fuck that bitch Tasha and her bastard son. Trent told me that Jamal don't claim that baby because Tasha is a known hoe." She said as we finished stuffing my stolen goods in the bags.

Dee Dee called a cab for me about a half hour went by and she handed me a twenty-dollar bill.

"Thank you Dee." I said hugging her.

"No problem you my lil sis Ima always look out." She said as the cab pulled up.

"Call me when you get home." she shouted just before the cab pulled off. I told the cab to let me out a block before my house because I didn't want my uncle or grandmother to see me getting out it I knew they would start hounding me with all types of questions in regards to my where a bouts and I didn't feel like the third degree because I was floating on cloud nine from my day out with Dee. Using my key, I opened the door and B-lined straight for my room to throw the bags into my closet. My grandmother was in her usual spot in the bed. These days she wasn't feeling too well.

"Hey grandma I'm home." She didn't acknowledge me she just turned towards the window.

"Do you need anything grandma?" Silence filled the space. I took that as a no and quietly closed her door and ran to my room to try on my new clothes. Everything fit perfect. It was amazing to me how fast Dee Dee grabbed all my right sizes right in front of me and how I didn't notice. The designer labels boosted my confidence as I tried on each piece one by one. There was no turning back I knew that from this day forward I would forever be clothed in nothing but the best. I bagged up all my old worn out gear and threw it on the back porch. I kept a few tee shirts and two pair of sweat pants just to lounge around the house in and replaced everything else with the new things I've acquired. In the mist of my new found high I almost forgot to call Dee Dee. I skipped to the kitchen grabbed the cordless, and retreated back to the confines of my bedroom to dial.

"Hello, bout time you called bitch." She answered in a sassy tone.

"My bad Dee I was lost in my own world trying on all my new gear you hooked me up with."

"Oh Lord I done created a monster but it's all good you're my lil monster." She joked. That made me giggled.

"Guess what D'Sire?"

"What?"

"It's on, Jamal is down to hook up this Saturday they on the phone planning our day as we speak." She squealed.

"Oh shit I forgot about the hook up. Desire did you hear me?"

"Yea I heard you that's what's up Dee." I said with forced excitement in my voice.

"Oooh girl I can't wait we gonna have so much fun Ima fuck the shit out of Trent." She added. Fear stuck me with a crippling force.

"Yea I can't wait either." I managed to push out.

"And girl I got the perfect plan, your grandmother will never notice you gone." Now she had my attention. She paused for what seemed like eternity.

"What?" I blurted.

"Oh my bad I just took a toke of the blunt."

"Would you just tell me?" I impatiently asked.

"It's easy you're going to drug her."

"Are you crazy I'm not drugging my grandmother." I yelled through the receiver forgetting for a brief moment that I was actually in her house.

"Dee Dee," I whispered, "I am not drugging my grandmother."

"Ok then Einstein, when you come up with a brilliant plan let me know." Her voice was full of sarcasm.

"Ok tell me what I got to do I said calmly."

"Well Trent was telling me about some stuff that you drop in the drink and it knocks the person out for almost 24 hours." She said with mystery in her voice.

"So how do you plan on getting that stuff from him?" I asked.

"I'm just going to tell him to get me some I'll make up something.

Girl you know I'm good at what I do. I got this damn, have some confidence in your girl."

"That's what I'm afraid of." I laughed.

"Afraid of what?" She asked.

"I'm afraid that this crazy plan of yours just might work."

"And when it does you can thank me later by naming you're first born by Jamal if it's a girl Diamond and Diamonique if it's a boy." She said. I felt her smiling through the phone.

"First of all I am not having any kids with Jamal and second of all I am not naming them after you that's why you so hot in da ass now because you were born with a stripper name." I teased.

"Oh really trick what about your name you're just a walking fuck fest waiting to happen." She retorted. Dee Dee had me on my bed hunched over in laughter; my stomach was hurting I tried to catch my breath.

"Alright hoe you fucking up my high I'm about to finish this blunt before my mother come home I'll see you tomorrow." She said.

"Ok talk to you later."

"Dee can I borrow some feet for Saturday?"

"Sure, what are you wearing?"

"I was thinking about the BCBG black stretch jeans with a black and silver fitted baby tee to match."

"Ok I got the perfect heels for you they're made by Chinese Laundry they fly as fuck fuck oh yea and I got a black and silver spiked belt for you to rock also." She said with much excitement in her voice.

"Tomorrow I think you should rock the Guess jeans. I will meet you at the bus stop with the cutest pair of red and white Jordan's you ever saw." She added.

"Ok I'll see you tomorrow then." I said and disconnected. Morning couldn't come any sooner. I was up and ready long before the first ray of sun had a chance to penetrate my window. I wore my hair pinned up in a doughnut bun. Curly tendrils formed around my hairline giving off on angelic halo that complemented my heart shape face. I glossed my full natural chrisom lips and grabbed my new Dooney & Burke book bag then hauled ass to the bus stop. Dee Dee was on time as promised with the red and white Jordans in tow. I switched from my dingy white classic Reeboks to the crisp comfort of the type of sneaker I only wore in my dreams. Now my whole ensemble was complete.

"Girl you looking fly as fuck!" Dee shrieked giving me dapp.

"Yea thanks to you," I said with a wide grin. "I've been trying to tell you D'Sire since I met you to get with the program. Aint you glad that you finally listened? Even though I had to trick yo ass to come with me. I just wanted to show you how easy it is and that there is nothing to be scarred of. My momma always said scarred money don't make no money. Yo I live and breathe that motto and apply it to everything I do. I go hard for mine and I want you to do the same thing no matter what. D'Sire you are beautiful you need to come out from under the rock and live your life you can't be stuck under your grandmother and uncle forever. Do you know how weird that is?" Although her last sentence almost made me laugh I could sense the sincerity in her voice.

"Thank you Dee Dee you have no idea how much this means to me."

"No problem D'Sire I just want you to see that you deserve the very best of everything no matter how you got to get it." She opened her hand.

"Look what I got." She said dropping a small clear valve with a black screw top in my hands.

"Oh shit this the stuff?" I asked in a hushed tone.

"Yupp Trent said he's not sure how much to use but I would think no more than four or five drops." She cautioned.

"Damn, I don't want to kill her I whispered."

"You aint gonna kill her just use a little try it tonight to see if it works k."

"Aight I'll see." I said and slipped the valve inside zipper of my bag. All day at school at kept checking it to see if the stuff was still there. I don't know where I expected it to go my bag never left my arm. I received tons of compliments on my new look also. Heads turned every time I entered a different room. Niggahs flocked and bitched was straight hating. Although a couple of the more popular ones did give me my props. I was enjoying all the attention it gave me a sense of power that I wasn't use to. After school I bolted to my bedroom to devise the plan. I figured my grandmother would be asleep around the usual time. I felt a lil bad for lying to Dee Dee because I really didn't think she needed to know all that. One thing that I've learned early on was never let the people close to you know your every move that was my motto I lived and breathed.

"D'Sire, come here." The sound of my uncle's voice boomed through my body causing my heart to stop. I closed my eyes and took in a deep breath.

"Here I come." I yelled after I composed myself.

## CHAPTER 13

"I need some pussy you still got your period?" He asked.

"No, I only spotted for two days."

"Go get me a beer and come give me some head."

I did as I was told while sliding the valve of stuff into my sneaker when I took them off. Uncle Jr. stood over me and unbuckled his pants letting them drop around his ankles then next his boxers and stepped out of them I looked up from my knelt position and took his swollen member into my mouth. He grabbed the back of my head forcing me to speed the rhythm. He grunted and his eyes began to roll in the back of his head. I knew he was about to bust. I sucked his dick allowing his erection to slip back and forth in my closed hand. My uncle pulled away.

"Ride me." I slid out my jeans and panties and hopped on his dick. "Yess baby ride this dick. Make uncle Jr. cum." I clenched my pussy muscles just like he taught me. "Ahhh D'Sire baby I'm about to cum oooh god." It was evident that my job was done. My uncle got up and used the bathroom. I seized the opportunity and slipped five drops of the stuff into his beer and swished it around. He came up behind me.

"What you doing?" I jumped.

"Nothing, I just wanted a sip of your beer." I said hoping he couldn't see the through the lie.

"Well get your own." He said pointing to the fridge.

"No problem." I said and popped the top off my own Budweiser. I took a long sip eyeing my uncle. He downed his beer straight back and let out a roaring belch.

"Get me another beer, yo why your pussy feels different?"

"Different like how?" I asked sensing some type of abuse brewing.

"You know how, come here." I sat my beer on the table. "Lay your ass down and open your legs." I followed his instructions.

"What uncle Jr?" Baam!

"Didn't I say lay yo stank ass the fuck down?" He had that look of rage. Blood trickled down my throat, I swallowed it afraid to move. My uncle roughly dug his fingers in my vagina scrapping the walls with his finger nails. I let out a cry as I felt the sting of torn inner flesh. He continued to scrape my insides until my body went numb. "Now bitch, that should teach you to give my pussy away." I jumped up and ran to the bathroom. Blood flowed from my nose and between my legs. I cleaned myself up sobbing at the same time. I wonder if this was my punishment for what I was about to do. When I entered back into the room the snore that came from my uncle confirmed that it was.

"Oh shit it worked!" I cried and laughed at the same time. I was delirious. I gathered my clothes and hauled ass to my room to call Dee Dee.

"Bitch it worked." I didn't have to say anything further she already knew what it meant.

"Ok D'Sire this is what you need to do, tomorrow stay in the house so you can see how long it takes to wear off. Do you remember what time you gave it?" she asked.

"Yea, about 15, minutes ago." I said.

"Ok, that was around 5:30 make sure you keep checking." She reiterated.

"I'm about to get up with Trent, he taking me to the movies. A hint of jealousy crept through me.

"Ok then I hope y'all have fun I'll talk to you tomorrow."

"D'Sire, make sure you call my cell phone if anything out of the ordinary happens."

"Girl, don't worry I got this." She laughed at me, because she knew I was mocking her. We disconnected. For the duration of the evening every hour on the hour I kept checking on uncle Jr. A couple times I got scared because it didn't sound like he was breathing but when I turned on the light I could see the rise and falls of his chest.

By the next morning I was getting more worried. I didn't want to call Dee Dee in fear of her catching me in a lie. I decided to wait for a few more hours to see what would happen. I was terrified because I wondered if my uncle would catch wind to what I've done to him. If he finds out I am as good as dead. I don't know why I let Dee Dee talk my dumb ass into doing this stupid shit. My uncle had me shitting bricks for 15 whole fucking hours. As soon as he woke up and saw my face he wanted some head. I sucked his dick really good. Deep throat style then prepared a dinner of fried chicken, corn and mashed potatoes for him. I dropped 5 more drops of that sleep potion in his beer again then sat with him making idol chat about school and a fake field trip to the museum of Natural History in New York that I wanted to go to and so on.

"Damn D'Sire I'm so tired. I think I need to take a few days off of work and you could take a couple days off from school to take good care of me."

"Sure, just let me know when." I tried to keep my tone up beat. He lightly caressed my nipple and instantly it became hard.

"I want some of that sweet pussy so bad but uncle Jr. is so fucking tired." He said as he staggered to the bed. I looked at the Lcd alarm clock it read 9:15 p.m. I still had plenty of time. So I shot upstairs and took a quick hot shower to relax my nerves. After my shower I lotioned up with my favorite Victoria Secret Pear scent that I stole from the mall and proceeded to get dress. The only thing missing was the belt and shoes but I wasn't worried because I knew Dee Dee was coming through for me. I dialed her cell phone.

"Hi D'Sire."

"Heyy girl. Everything is all set I'm ready." I nervously said.

"Calm down we'll be there in about 10 minutes, be looking out because Ima have Trent turn off the head lights when we pull up."

"Ok I'll be waiting bye." I whispered. I decided to wear my natural curly hair down for the evening. I added a little grease and water to it to loosen them up and raked my fingers through until I was satisfied with the way it felt. I stuffed my book bag with a pair of boy shorts and a wife beater to sleep in and some extra toiletries. I crept down to the basement to check on uncle Jr. Thankfully he was still knocked out. I left the back porch unlocked so I could sneak back in the house and waited in stealth under the cloak of darkness for Trent's car to pull up. Several minutes dragged. My nerves found a new breading ground in the back of my throat, causing tingles of fear to shoot out my heart in frenzied palpitations. For some strange reason it seemed like my house was darker than usual. It held all my secrets and beckoned me to return to the safety of its confines. I seriously contemplated the notion until the slow approach of Trent's car snapped me out of my reverie. I emerged from the side of the house and quickly approached the car. Jamal opened the door for me from the inside. I climbed into the back seat Trent pulled off quickly as I as I shut the door.

"Hey yall what's poppin?" I said greeting the trio.

"What's up D'Sire, you look nice." Jamal said.

"Thank you Jamal." My response was introverted.

"Girl I had to do a double take when you rolled up on us from them bushes looking like a high fashion ninja." She joked, "But you wearing those jeans." She complimented, discreetly handing over the bag which contained my belt and shoes. I slipped into the black and silver heels and quickly looped my belt damn there all in one motion. Trent was quiet as he drove; every now and then I would catch him intensely eyeing me in the rearview.

"You smoke?" Jamal asked pulling a tightly wrapped blunt from his ear. He lit it and extended it towards me as if he already knew the answer.

"No doubt." I said smiling carefully pinching it between my thumb and pointer fingers. I placed the open end to my lips and deeply inhaled then blew all my troubles away with the smoke. Instantly my body went into relax mode.

"That's what's up I love a woman who can smoke with her man and handle if you know what I mean."

"Wait, did he just say woman?"

"Yea that's the epitome of sexy if you ask me." He continued. We arrived at our destination the Red Roof Inn in Milford. Trent pulled to the entrance. He and Jamal both exited the car and went inside. Dee Dee turned to me with an expression on her face that beamed with excitement.

"Girl, you better work it on Jamal tonight this some exclusive shit they took us to so you know he gonna want some ass." She said.

"Don't worry trick I got this." I said with a slight neck roll. The weed had me feeling loose and my pussy felt wet.

"Damn D'Sire I'm ready to get fucked so bad I wish they come they asses on." She said passing the blunt back to me. The guys came back to the car all smiles.

"We parked in the rear of the hotel. We got lucky and I got two rooms right next to each other." Jamal said. Trent popped the trunk and both he and Jamal walked to the back of the car. They emerged with two large bags one in each of their hands. We walked up two flights of stairs. Trent led the way and Jamal was last behind me. We stopped in front of a red door with gold metal numbers that read 219. Dee Dee and Trent's room was 220. We all entered our perspective quarters. Once inside I was able to get a better look at Jamal. He had on a long dark blue tee with yellow cursive script that read FUBU across the chest and FUBU denim jeans that sagged a little he rocked blue and white Jordans and his Yankee fitted was crisp. His 18 carat gold Cuban link chain adorned his neck hanging low past his navel with a diamond encrusted white Jesus piece attached.

"You know how to play pool D'Sire?"

"I don't know I've never played." I truthfully stated.

"Come on Ima teach you." He said grabbing my hand.

"Should I tell Dee we leaving?" I asked caught off guard by the sudden change of plans.

"Nawww you straight Ma I aint gonna kidnap you unless you want me to." He joked displaying well-kept teeth. I laughed even though I was still a little nervous yet still I followed him downstairs. I heard a car alarm disarm and the headlights of a triple black Cadillac Escalade flashed. The chrome rims it sat on sparkled like stars contrasting across a clear pitch black sky. Jamal opened the passenger door. I just stood still.

"Ma this me. I met Trent here earlier and parked. It didn't make sense to bring both vehicles to pick you up." He explained.

"Oh." I let out sigh of relief suddenly feeling my age again. I was a little embarrassed by my actions. I composed myself and climbed in the massive truck. Jamal closed the door behind me. We pulled out of the parking lot and drove 95 North towards New Haven. Ruff Ryders Anthem video popped on the LCD screen in the console and on the four other screens in the headrests. "I know a spot we can go to where they don't card."

He said while concentrating on the road. I kept quiet because I had no idea what he was talking about and I didn't want to have another episode. We continued to drive for about 15 minutes until finally we reached our destined spot. All types of cars lined the street from Benzes to Beamers and a few big body trucks like Jamal's. My body felt all tingly and when I walked the friction created a heightened sense of arousal in between my legs. We entered the building. Jamal handed a muscular bald man two ten dollar bills. The man took the money and began to pat him down like a police officer would do a suspect. I turned around for him to do me next but instead he just ushered us in. Once inside the pulse of the music ran though my body sending electricity through my veins. I felt good beyond measure. The lights dimmed.

"Coming to the stage is the beautiful sensuous sex kitten Perrsia!" The unseen announcer's voice boomed through the system that surrounded the bar. Colorful lights began to flash and the most beautiful woman I've ever saw entered the stage area. She wore a vinyl stretched, cat suit that looked like black liquid on her skin. Her full D cup breast stood at attention and looked sexy against her hour glass figure. She was of Asian and Black decent and her hair was straight, jet black down to the top of her curvy ass. She hypnotized me with the way she gyrated her hips to prince's song Darling Nicky. Men and women both hurled all denominations of bills on the stage.

"You like her huh." Jamal whispered in my ear sending my pussy into a pulsing frenzy.

"Yess." I said never taking my eyes off her. Jamal left for several minutes returning with a fist full of bills. He sat at a table facing close to the stage at arm's reach of the dancer.

"Come sit on my lap D'Sire." I did as I was told. Immediately the woman made eye contact with me and strolled to where we were seated. Jamal handed me an undisclosed amount of money and told me to make her work for it. I held a handful of bills over her as she got on her knees clapping her ass for us. I hurled the bills in the air and they landed all over the stage. The crowd went bananas. A topless waitress in a white thong strolled to our table. As soon as the black light hit it her thong glowed in a hypnotic blue color.

"What would you two like to drink?" She asked looking directly at Jamal.

"I'll take a Hennessey straight and a Heineken. D'Sire?"

"I'll have the same." The waitress was back in a flash. Jamal gave her a 50.00-dollar bill and told her to keep the change. She kept the drinks flowing for the rest of the night. When the stripper came out, I was attracted to her until she finished her set, then she disappeared into the dressing room. The DJ announced the next dancer. An attractive bleach blond Caucasian woman with huge fake titties and petite frame entered the stage. She had a banging tan and piercing blue sparkling eyes. Her choice of music was a classic Guns n Roses song. I kept a watchful eye on the dressing room door. The cat woman emerged wearing a long skin tight halter style gown with a side split that came up to the top of her thigh, she appeared goddess like. Her clear stiletto heels gave off a Cinderella glass slipper type of illusion. Her walk was fierce like a runway model. She beeline to our table.

"Hey Jamal, who's your friend?" She asked licking her luscious glossed lips.

"Persia D'Sire, D'Sire Persia." He said as she and I locked eyes. She broke her stare first.

"Jamal you got the goods?"

"Baby you know I got you." He said placing six pink star shaped candy looking things in her open palm. She popped one in her mouth and took a sip of Jamal's beer.

"These the same ones from last time right?" She said more like an assumption than a question. Jamal nodded. Persia whispered something in Jamal's ear he threw his head back and laughed.

"Persia wants to give you a lap dance D'Sire." Persia took my hand into hers and led me to a private section in the back of the club. She gave the huge man that stood guard over the area a discrete nod and he unhooked the black velvet rope that separated the room. She pulled the heavy opaque, red drape to the side allowing me to enter first. The room's furniture was eccentric in design. A hand painted black and gold table with a fishbowl full of condoms sat In between two leopard print chairs in the shape of a woman's high heal. A round bed with custom fitted leopard print sheets sat atop a black wood platform. Persia caught me staring at the bed.

"Don't worry honey, the sheets get changed after every session." she assured. Tea light candles were strategically placed around the room.

"Sit down on the bed D'Sire, relax I'm going to take care of you." She said giving me an intense look. Persia sat close to me. Her hand delicately brushed the side of my face then through my hair. I closed my eyes and, I parted my lips slightly to suck in oxygen causing my chest to rise. She leaned in and kissed me slow and deep. I welcomed her advance. Our tongues tangoed in exotic rhythm, tasting clean and sweet when they met.

She systematically pulled my shirt off over my head then unsnapped my bra. Once my breast was free she popped both my cinnamon swirl nipples in her mouth, then one at a time back and forth paying them both equal attention. In one swift movement she had me out of my jeans and panties.

"Lay back D'Sire." I obeyed. Her fingers explored my body until they found the juicy folds of my ripe pussy. She ran them softly in between the opening of my swollen lips while continuing to suck on my breast, then slowly moved down to my stomach planting soft kisses to my inner thighs sucking with more intensity. An uncontrolled cry of passion escaped my lips once her mouth found its mark. She drilled her tongue deep in and out then vibrated my clit with speeds of rapid apportions. I called out to god from the waves of pleasure that escaped my body. Persia kissed me again in the mouth and I slid down to the moist opening of her vagina and sucked and licked like my life depended on it. Her smell was intoxicating she pulled my hair.

"Oh god D'Sire, yess!" She screamed as she climaxed. She tasted sweet. Next she lay in between my legs. There is no level of expression on this earthly plane that can equate to what I felt the moment our clits met for the first time.

## CHAPTER 14

I had no idea what time we got back to the room or how. All I do know is I awoke in the arms of Jamal and we were both butt ass naked.

"Damn I don't know if I fucked this niggah or what." I said to myself. Little did I know at the time that this was only the beginning stage of many more episodes to come. The previous night was one big head pounding blur. Bits and pieces would flash before me, yet I still couldn't decipher so I just gave up because it hurt too much to try. The only thing I did remember in detail was me and Dee Dee smoking a blunt.

"Yo ma, you a beast off the X." Jamal said getting out of the bed. I had no idea what the hell he was talking about.

"Ugh I feel like shit." I said as I dragged myself to the toilet to throw up. My body violently jerked as it projected thick, slimly, yellow bile from the hollows of my empty stomach.

"Go ahead let it out." He coaxed as my mouth salivated warning me that another episode was approaching. Jamal rubbed my back and placed a cold wash cloth on my face.

"My head hurts badly." I said after puking my brains out.

"That's because when your pupils are dilated for a period of time, too much light filters in causing a headache." He expertly explained sounding more like a doctor. He placed two white oblong shaped pills in my palm and a Dixie cup of cold tap water in the other.

"Take these you'll feel better." My gag reflex kicked into overdrive as I chugged the pills down my throat. I was too spent to ask questions all I wanted was the bed. I began to crawl in the direction but my attempt was intercepted with Jamal's strong arms carrying me instead. Darkness enveloped me as my soul drifted away. I later discovered that my semi drug induced black out was caused by an illegal substance called ecstasy. Without my knowledge, Jamal laced the weed that night with the crush pills and the side effect of the drug sent my body into shock. I had to stay out a whole extra night so I could stabilize and paid the ultimate price as I tried to sneak back into the house.

"Oh my god uncle Jr. You scarred the shit out of me." I nervously said after flicking on my bedroom light. He was sitting on my bed smoking a Newport. An empty half gallon of Seagrams Gin lay next to him. His blood shot eyes held the fury of a mad man as they cut into my soul. Instinctively I took two steps back.

"I'm a ask you one mutha fuckin time and one time only and if you even think about lying to me Ima kill you D'Sire." His eyes narrowed and he was sweating.

"Where the fuck you been all day? The school called and left a message saying you aint show up." He said as he slowly rose to his feet. I could smell the stench of liquor permeate from his pours.

"Uncle Jr. I-- I --- was with Dee Dee." I stammered.

"With Dee Dee where bitch?" He vehemently spat. With lightning speed, he lunged at me and I turned to run towards the kitchen but he caught me winding my hair three times around his tightly closed hand.

"No please uncle Jr. I promise please oh god noo!" I begged as he dragged me from the kitchen and down the basement stairs. The cold cement floor greeted me with a bone crushing blow as I landed on all fours. My knees shattered on impact, I screamed in agony. I heard a loud tree branch like snap followed by an excruciating sharp pain as his steel toe construction boot landed on my side my screams were silence by a second then a third blow. I began to suffocate. I was now on my back gasping for air. My lungs were scorched. I knew I was about to die and broken body spasmed in horror as I watched him reach into his dip and display a chrome 9mm semi-automatic hand gun.

"Didn't I promise yo stankin ass a long time ago that if you ever gave my pussy away I would kill you?" He growled spitting hot liquor breath with every syllable. I shook my head yes eyes wide with horror. He dragged me by my hair pulling it tight forcing me into a semi standing position with my neck yanked back. Then with the butt of the gun he knocked me onto the bed and roughly turned me on my stomach. Warm blood flowed into my eye with stinging blindness as it gushed out of the gaping wound above it. My uncle then grabbed his switch blade tearing my flesh as he shredded my clothes off of me. For a brief moment he left me alone but I was paralyzed by fear unable to move I could not save myself. He soon returned with a jar of Vaseline. I heard a deep moan of pleasure escape from him. Then I felt the cold steel of the gun against the back of my head. Suddenly without warning he jammed his fully erected penis into my anus severing its skin, violently pounding it in and out. My body convulsed and his laugh was of wicket nature. He began to grunt loudly as he displayed animalistic behavior in my anal canal. As he reached his climax I heard him scream.

"I love you D'Sire!" Followed by two loud pops, I felt intense heat in the back of my head then the weight of his body as he slumped on me. My life flashed before me as I took my last breath.

## CHAPTER 15

Present

I awoke much later than anticipated so immediately I hauled ass to the bathroom to handle my business. Once out of the shower I threw on my black BeBe skinny leg stretch jeans with matching tee, and a cute pair of zebra print Michael Kors flats that I coped last week from Nordstrom's. My mind wandered as I casually scrolled through the miss call and text list on my cell phone. I thought about how much my life has changed dramatically over the past few years and how I've evolved despite of all I've been through. An E-mail blast from Monica caught my eye. It said that R&B artist Sincere was recording at 50 cent's Connecticut mansion and she immediately wanted me on assignment. It went on to say that she pre-arranged a meeting at Nitro, a night club in Bridgeport, because he was the celebrity judge in the battle rappers contest. There was no way of getting out of this so I sent Monica a confirmation that I've received the message.

A few seconds later she texted, "tonight 7:30 pm sharp." along with a telephone number and the owners name. I then transferred the info into my contacts list and dialed.

"Nitro Tonya speaking."

"Hello is Chaz available?"

"He's busy who's this?" She asked unprofessionally.

"My name is D'Sire I represent Street Talk Magazine could you please…"

"Hold on."

"Um hi this is Chaz."

"Hi Chaz my name is D'Sire. I received an email about the battle rappers event and that you would like some promotion for your club in exchange for an interview with the celebrity guest judge, Sincere correct." I said strategically yet in a professional manor.

"Well uhh yea that's cool how soon can you come down?" He asked catching the bait.

"How about 7:30 pm?"

"Ok, do you know how to get here?"

"Yes I have the directions programmed in my phone already."

"That's what's up so I will see you at 7:30 then and your name again?"

"D'Sire."

"Aight D'Sire I'll see you at 7:30 then."

"Ok Chaz I will text you when I'm on my way." We disconnect. Part of my job was my ability to be available at any given moment and use tactical measures when it came to securing an exclusive interview such as this. I texted my boss to let her know I'm covering the story and later I will email her an outline of the interview along with pictures.

She texted back, "great job I knew I could count on you." Those words of praise made me smile. I continued to scroll through my messages.

"Hi, D'Sire I just want to thank you for last night and to let you know that Dominick called to say that he will be available to take me where I need to go so I guess this means your free to enjoy your day and I will call you later to let you know if we had any luck finding anything ok TTYL." That was cool with me because there was a diversion in my plans anyway so it all worked out I opened the sliding door that led to the patio and decide to kill time constructively by researching the artist to be interviewed. With the help of my favorite search engine I was able to write down all his stats to formulate my own distinct questions for the article and as a bonus I wrote a brief out line on the history of battle rapping along with separate questions for the club's owner. Satisfied with my work I closed the screen and opened the untitled file in Word that I started and began where I left off. All kinds of emotion began to surface as my fingers automatically stroked each key without conscious thought. I lost all sense of time as I became totally engrossed with this newly discovered writing style I've acquired. Suddenly I stopped and realized when I began to read that I had written the first nine pages of my life's story. A sickening feeling twisted inside my gut. I clutched my stomach running to the bathroom to release the bitter tasting bile into the toilette. My knees felt loose and my hand shook and rattled the cold silver handle as it weakly flushed all the poison of my past in one big swirl down the porcelain hole that waited. I stood staring into the empty toilet as if waiting for its opinion on what it just tasted but of course there were none. So I used the sink as support to rise into a full standing position and caught a glimpse of myself in the mirror. My skin was clammy, void of color and my eyes looked hollow. I splashed cold water on my face and when I looked in the mirror again I clutched my chest in horror from the image of my uncle Jr. His face distorted dripping with thick dark clotted blood.

"D'Sire I'm coming for you." He reached out to me. I screamed hysterically turning around but he was gone. I looked in the mirror then again behind me. He really wasn't there. No blood on the floor, nothing I trembled and faced the bathroom door as I brushed my teeth and gargled. My soul leaped from my body leaving me stiff as T-Roy's ring tone Sex Scenario blared through the speaker of my Black Berry. Still visibly shaken I answered barely audible.

"Hello."

"D'Sire is that you?"

"Yes Troy it's me."

"Is everything alright? You sound different."

"Yea everything is fine I'm just a lil tired. Up all night trying to catch up on some overdue work that's all." I said trying to fix my voice.

"What's going on with you?" I asked changing the subject.

"Still in the studio everything is going well with the tracks. I called to invite you up to help me with a song. For you know some inspiration." I knew exactly what he meant by that.

"I can't tonight Troy."

"Why not?" I sensed disappointment in his voice.

"Because, Monica has me on assignment."

"Oh yea, where at?"

"At this sports bar in Bridgeport called Nitro. They have a battle rappers contest going on and there's a celebrity judge named Sincere who is attending so she wants the write up in next month's issue I'm sorry." I apologized. It's aight ma I respect your grind. I heard good things about that cat Sincere I like his style. Maybe you could put in a good word for me and we could collaborate on something."

"That shouldn't be a problem I'll do my best to plug you in."

"I miss your sexy ass." He said switching subjects.

"I miss you too Troy." I truthfully stated. The sound of his deep voice gave me a sense of comfort, I no longer felt threatened even though he was miles away. Besides I realized that what I imagined I saw was just my mind playing tricks on me because I entered into a past that I vowed to forget and it just had to remind me why.

"So what's up with tomorrow? I can send a car for you and we could go out then drive back to your place together."

"That sounds like a good idea I'm down."

"Aight then I guess I have to wait till tomorrow to see my baby." He said as if he was talking to a third party. I could just imagine the look on his face. The thought of it made me smile inward.

"Ok Troy I'll see you tomorrow then."

"Oh D'Sire call me later to let me know how the interview went."

"No problem I'll be up all night editing anyways I could take some time out for you."

"Aight baby I'll talk to you later then."

"Ok Troy." I pushed the end button on my phone. The creepy feeling, I felt earlier was trying to emerge from its confines so I grabbed my gun out the night stand and carefully put it in my oversized black Prada, retrieved my car keys off the living room table and bolted out the front door to do some therapeutic shopping. I felt like company so I dialed Sasha.

"Hold on D'Sire, let my hang up with this trick." There was a brief a pause.

"Hello." He answered

"Hi Sasha did I catch you at a wrong time?"

"No girl as a matter of fact your call was right on time. That was nobody but Dan's sorry ass trying to make up an excuse to why his car wasn't in front of his house after three in the morning. Honey please I went straight ballistic on his cheating ass. I know what time the fuckin club closes." He ranted.

"Sounds like you need to spend the day with me." I said with slight hope in my voice.

"Girl what you getting into?"

"I figured we could meet up at Party Nation then hit the mall…"

"Bitch say no more I'll be there. What time are you talking?"

"How about now" I said hoping he wouldn't peep my desperation.

"Bitch you're lucky I love you give me about an hour I have to take Peaches out to tinkle."

"Ok no problem I'll be waiting ciao."

"Smooches." He said and popped his lips before disconnecting. I continued my drive to Party Nation and braced myself for the earful I was most definitely about to receive. Sasha pulled up behind me in his black and silver two seater Porsche beeping wildly. I automatically rolled my eyes at the dramatic scene he displayed.

"D'Sire, I have to wait for two spaces because I don't want anyone parking near me." He whined.

"Sasha what's the point in having such a nice car and not being able to enjoy it, just park bitch. You had me waiting for almost two hours." I said clearly displaying aggravation.

"Well I had to stay behind a lil longer because Peaches had an anxiety attack because she knew that I was leaving the house and I had to calm her and give her the psyche meds her doggie psychiatrist prescribed. Oh god it was horrible I had to hold her over the toilet because she kept throwing up D'Sire it was quite a scene." I could not help but to forgive him after hearing all that.

"Sasha you and Peaches are both a mess." I said laughing. "Now go park so we can shop for my party." He pulled off and several minutes later met me inside the huge outlet.

"You look cute." I honestly complimented. He had on faded washed Express Jeans with the perfect amount of shred on the left thigh and back pockets, a black form fitted tee that read AX in white letters and black Armani flip flop showed off perfect manicured toes. His black designer sunglasses adorned the top of his head crowning plump jet black god given curls. I could honestly see why he had no choice but to be gay because he was too pretty, too perfect not to be.

"D'Sire, he stated seriously. Does it look like my butt got bigger?" He asked tooting his ass clearly wanting me to say that it did.

"Yes Sash your ass is getting bigger." I played along. We walked over to the registration desk.

"Hi how may we help you today?" An average looking middle aged white woman asked.

"Ah yes my friend here D'Sire would like a party consultant to show her a few of your most glamour's entertainment themes that you have available. Sasha said on my behalf.

"Ok sure we can arrange that. Do you have an appointment?" She asked turning towards me.

"Uh, no I wasn't aware that I had to, it did not state that on your web site."

"Well yea that's our policy but you are free to take a look around you might find some nice things on your own." The woman went on to say.

"Look lady. Sasha stepped in. If we just wanted to take a look around, we would have shopped online. Where is your manger? I need to speak to the manger right now." He raved, creating a scene.

"No sir that won't be necessary I'll just check in the system to see if there is a cancellation." She said turning a shade of chrisom.

"Well you should have just done that in the first place." Sasha angrily retorted with his hands on his hip. I just look at Sasha's dramatic ass and shook my head when the lady suddenly found us a time slot only 10 minutes away.

"Please take a seat and fill out this form. One of our consultants will be right over to assist you momentarily." She said through a clenched smile.

## CHAPTER 16

Sasha and the party consultant Angel, hit it off well. He too was gay and definitely Sasha's type. He was tall tan and athletically built he had low cropped cut dark hair and a sense of style that smelled of money. He told us that he attended the New York Institute of Design and once he finished his parents were giving him his own party planning business as a graduation present next year. He and Sasha exchanged phone numbers on the low as I handed the cashier my credit card.

"Ok miss D'Sire, I will be at your place on Aug 13th a day before the party to access the place then I will return on the 14th to set everything up around 5:00 pm. Also I will be working with a crew of six we will be dropping off all the food beverages and party gifts on that Friday. What is a convenient time for your dear?"

"Noon is fine."

"Ok will do." He said adding information into his Black Berry.

"Ooh I just love what I do." He sang truly excited.

"Now that is money well spent." Sasha said grabbing the receipt out of my hand pointing to the two thousand seventy-three-dollar total. I agreed with him because it eased my mind knowing that all the details would be professionally handled and I didn't have to do all the running around. I left Party Nation with a feeling of confidence that everything was going to turn out perfect. Sasha and I hit up a local mall and shopped in our favorite luxury department stores until hunger and exhaustion finally kicked in we decided to eat at Captain Galley, a seafood restaurant in West Haven near the beach. We both ate king crab legs, steamed, clams and fresh arugula pesto salad. We also enjoyed a few mid-day cocktails. The after work crowd was beginning to nosily shuffle in for happy hour to patronize the bar area for spicy buffalo wings and drink specials as we were leaving.

"D'Sire, I had a fabulous time with you girl. We definitely have to do this again soon." He said giving me air smooches first on the left then the right side of my cheeks.

"I'm so excited about your party and I can't wait to see how everything's going to turn out. You have such good taste too I just love the color scheme you chose so retro glam." He added.

"Thanks Sash, I had fun too and I appreciate the recommendation."

"No problem D'Sire you know I got your back. Oh and what is this I hear about you securing a major interview?" He managed to sneak in. *Wow news travel fast. I knew Monica couldn't keep it to herself I thought.*

"Oh yea speaking of, I really have to go, I need to get home and shower. Sash I'll text you tonight and give you all the details."

"Promise." He asked raising one perfect arched brow.

"Yes Sasha, I give you my word." I assured.

"Ok trick you are free to go. I'll see you at work Monday. Take care D'Sire."

"You too." I responded and headed for my car. I showered, changed clothes and headed back out. It would take approximately twenty minutes to reach my destination. Traffic was mild and I was way ahead of schedule. The ravishing sun blazed like a ball of reddish orange brilliance as it began its decent into the horizon. I donned my platinum and ivory tusk Channel frames and sucked my teeth wondering why they invented the sun visor because it served no purpose what so ever. I dialed Chaz and immediately put the call on speaker before the first ring.

"Nitro." He answered right away I recognized the authority on the other end.

"Hi Chaz this is D'Sire. Just calling to let you know that I'm on my way."

"Ok ma, when you get here just pull around the back. What you pushing so I could have my peoples escort you?"

"A white Benz."

"Aight then I'll see you when you get here drive safe."

"Ok thank you." I replied before disconnecting the call. I drove for about fifteen minutes more before exiting the ramp. When I arrived there was a tall dark skin guy with a low Caesar cut that stood in front of the bar smoking a Newport. He was mean muggin when I rolled up and his expression quickly transformed to a sexy Tyreese kind of squint once my passenger side tinted window whirled down. He took one last drag of his cigarette then plucked it at an impressive distance before approaching my car.

"Hi I'm supposed to meet with Chaz." I said removing my shades.

"God dam!" He exclaimed "You must be D'Sire. You're a writer for Street Talk?" He asked in a somewhat questionable tone mixed with shock.

"Yea why?" I asked on the defense.

"Because Ma you blazing as hell we all was expecting some geek looking chick to come rolling up in here but dam no disrespect you are model material. We should be doing the story on you."

His words were flattering. "So where should I park?" I asked changing the subject.

"Oh my bad make a U-turn and park in the back next to the black BMW." I followed his instructions before I could put my shift gear in park dude was on the driver's side ready to open the door. I was obliged by the gesture and before securing my vehicle I grabbed my purse and popped the trunk to retrieve my briefcase.

"My name Marquise, me and my mans June work the door at Nitro." He handed me a business card.

"I also own a barbershop on Boston ave. I help my boy Chaz out on weekends because this place be packed." I observed the six luxury cars in the lot.

"Oh trust ma I peep the look on your face. You'll see, it's early. It's a good thing you came now because once the crowd gets here you won't be able to hear yourself think." He said convincingly as a silent laugh shook through his body. Marquise led the way and held the side door open so I entered first. A pretty thick light skinned chick with a long kept weave, slanted eyes and voluptuous breast stood behind the well-stocked bar. I felt the salt she threw towards me a she sucked her teeth when we approached.

"Tonya this is D'Sire. D'Sire, Tonya." Marquise said introducing us unfazed by her rudeness.

"Hi." she dryly said without eye contact.

"Marquise how long is this interview pose to be?" She questioned.

"I don't know ask your man." He responded. Oh I see jealous girlfriend. Marquise need to give his boy Chaz some advice on teaching his woman how to conduct herself in a business setting I thought to myself. Then I smiled inward as my old ways began to slither inside because this bitch really had no clue on how I get down and if she fucks with me tonight Ima give her every reason to really question her self-worth. One thing I hate most in this world is an insecure bitch. I simply brushed my shoulder off because I was here to do a job and I had to keep rivet on what mattered most and that was securing this interview which was definitely going to boost my career up a few notches. I refused to waste much needed energy on this hating ass antagonist who shot invisible daggers my way.

"Marquise where's Chaz?" I beamed.

"He stepped out for a minute do you want something to eat or a drink?

"He asked. I thought about it then declined. I would not give this bitch the pleasure of spitting in my shit.

"Let me show you around." He suggested. Tonya slit her eyes at me.

"Nice meeting you Tonya." I said throwing her my signature smile while tossing my hair over my shoulder. Hate leaped from her pours which added more stench to her already stinking ass attitude. If she acts like this with competition in the room around Marquise I can only imagine the monster she becomes around her man.

"Don't mind Tonya she acts like this whenever she isn't the center of attention." Marquise said once we were out of ear shot. There were a few wood square tables that seated four scattered in the next room which was adjacent to the bar area, and an open space which I assume was so people could dance. Opposite to that room was a half sheet rock type wall which separated this room from the DJ booth and pool table. I looked around wondering where I was supposed to conduct the interview. Marquise must have picked up on my vibe he led me through a hallway that had a brown square table and two chairs.

"This is where you're going to talk to Sincere at." He said pointing to the table. It was evident that we were next to both the men's and women's bathroom. I stood stuck for about a minute.

"Oh." Is all I said this isn't quite what I expected but it would have to do, it's all about the interview, I said to myself. I think my expression gave my inner thoughts away.

"You got to excuse the place Chaz is the middle of renovating. This use to be Tito's he bought it as is. There are two big rooms in the back but they are filled with the previous owner's things. Chaz is making those into VIP rooms once he cleans them out he's going to remodel em."

"Oh I see." Marquises loyalty towards Chaz was like armor. He went through great lengths to explain everything in detail about the establishment to me and make me feel comfortable. The sound of glass breaking jolted us out of conversation and, I trailed behind Marquise as he bolted towards the bar area. Voices were raised. It sounded like Tonya was having a heated argument with somebody.

"You no good motha fucka I know you fuckin that bitch!"

"What you talking about Tonya she here to interview Sincere. I told you about that jealous shit man you always trying to fuck up something for me."

"Fuck you niggah and that bitch I'm about to take you for everything you got. I'm leaving and I'm taking lil Chaz with me!" She screamed. Chaz grabbed Tonya by the back of her neck just in time as she lunged at me with a broken Heineken bottle it slipped out of her hand shattering into thousands of jagged fragments on impact. I remained collected as my hand automatically stroked the weapon concealed in my bag.

"Yo Marquise hold it down man I'll be right back" Chaz said still gripping Tonya by the neck.

"Bitch when I see you in the street I'm a beat that ass!" She spat full of venom.

"D'Sire, I am so sorry you had to see that I told Chaz that girl was not wifey material and to top it off he stuck because he got a seed with her." Marquise shook his head clearly disappointed.

"I respect you D'Sire; I can't believe how calm you were even when she came at you with that bottle." He added clearly amazed. If he only knew how close, I came to busting a cap in that bitch ass he would take those words back.

"What's good? I just dammed there got ran over by Chaz." A tall slim nice looking guy said upon entering. He walked with a slight limp as he approached us giving marquise dap. A dark skin dude with neatly kept dreads followed suit.

"Daam, this you Quise?" He added with assumption not a question.

"Naww man I wish she was, she's the one doing the interview with Sincere, and Tonya jealous ass tried to cut her with a bottle for no reason dawg. Her name D'Sire, D'Sire this my boy June and that fake ass Jamaican over there is Tron." He said pointing at the dread. Tron nodded he looked stuck, high as hell. I glanced at my BlackBerry.

"It's almost that time." I said. "You know what Marquise I think I'll have that drink now." I said taking a seat at the bar. I needed something to calm my nerves.

"How about a Hennessey and coke?" I said. June and Tron ordered Heinekens. Marquise made my drink and grabbed three beers out the ice bucket. He popped his top with a lighter.

"Y'all niggahs can open your own beers. I got to clean this mess up that bitch made." he said clearly heated. June and I conversed he wanted to know everything regarding my field of work. And was quite animated as I went into detail answering all questions he hammered me with. I was under the impression that he thought I was like some type of Barbara Walters or something. He kept referring me to her. I didn't mind I took it as his way of paying me a compliment June was cool. His boy Tron was very reserved. They were totally opposite of one another. Chaz entered the bar area with Sincere, I knew who he was from all the Googling I've done earlier. He was very handsome even more so in person.

"D'Sire, I apologize for earlier." Chaz said looking embarrassed.

"Apology accepted." I assured.

"Marquise explained briefly what you two are going through so I understand. In my line of work anything can happen so I tend to expect the unexpected." I said flashing a smile.

"We didn't get to formally meet. I'm Chaz and this is my good friend, Sincere." I extended my hand to each of them.

"Nice to meet the both of you, my name is D'Sire."

## CHAPTER 17

Marquise excused himself.

"D'Sire it was nice meeting you, I got to go work the door. I will be in touch I would like to do some advertising for my shop in the magazine."

"Nice meeting you too Marquise, thank you for showing me around and keeping me company I'll be waiting for that call. Oh hold on before you go I need to get a picture with you. Chaz if you don't mind could you take our picture please?" I said retrieving my Sony digital camera from its case, then handing it to him.

"Just push right here." I said pointing to the silver button on the top.

"Don't worry the camera self-adjusts on its own." I handed Marquise our most recent issue of Street Talk and we posed together in front of the bar. He held the magazine with the cover facing the camera in his right hand and placed his left arm behind my back around my waist and I learned towards him.

"Yall ready?" Chaz asked looking into the lens. I nodded and the camera's flash lit up the room. Chaz gave me back the camera confused by all the buttons. I scrolled through until we popped up on the screen.

"This is a nice picture of us." I said showing Marquise. Everyone gathered around even Tron for their turn to flick it up next. I passed a small spiral notebook around.

"Make sure you guys put in a contact number or email address so I can send you a copy of the pictures. First my editorial team back at the office have to pick out the ones they want and as soon as they get published I will send them to you Ok."

"That's what's up." Tron said. We all paused for a moment.

"Let me find out Ima have to start walking around here with a camera to get your ass to talk niggah." June jokes. We all laughed.

"Nawww for real just the other day I told him how that shoot out went down in Ricco's Mini mart on the Ave and how I almost got killed trying to order a sub and all this niggah could do was nod, I'm saying we been boys since high school and I can't remember not one conversation with him." he added.

"That's because both yall niggahs stay high. June you be like Tron you want to smoke? And Tron just nod his head that's yall conversation every day all day. I be with yall niggahs so I know." Marquise said.

"Yea but how come today is the first time I noticed?" June asked looking serious like he really been enlightened.

"I don't know niggah maybe the camera flash woke your brain cells up." Chaz said cracking up it was going on eight o'clock

I wrote down a few instructions for Chaz to delegate so this interview could flow easy. I needed him to give me a list of all contestants in the battle rappers contest plus I wanted him to reserve a spot where patrons of the bar could leave email address so I could network with them at a later time. Also I needed him to place Street Talk Magazines and my business cards throughout the establishment so people could pick up at random. I excused myself and told Chaz that I needed to start the interview. Sincere and I walked through the hallway where the table stood and we both sat down. He appeared to be very comfortable. It was clear to me that he's been here before and he already knew what to expect. His demeanor was smooth and poised. He was a southern gentleman easy to talk to. He explained to me that the previous label he was signed to screwed him and how he was starting over on his own and he went on to tell me briefly about his childhood and what inspires him most to sing. We talked about future endeavors and a little about how he met Fifty Cent. No matter how hard I tried Sincere would not disclosed any information about the project he and Fifty were collaborating on and as a journalist I had to respect that. I pressed the off button on my mini recorder. "Sincere, I need to ask you something off the record. I usually wouldn't do this but the person who asked me is a close friend of mine. You probably heard his music on the radio. His name is T-Roy he wants to know if you would like to work with him on a few songs."

"Yea I like his style that song Lonely Star is off the chain." He said Sincere and I exchanged numbers. I also gave him T-Roy's information. He quickly transferred everything into his BlackBerry as I spoke.

"Ok thank you for the interview I'm pretty sure our readers will appreciate the invitation into your life." I said standing.

"No problem. Are you staying to watch the show?" He asked.

"Of course I am and plus I need to talk to the contestants and interview the winner." I said popping a fresh tape into my recorder.

"Then I'll be sure to catch up with you before you slide." He said

"Oh trust I'll be the one hunting you down for more pictures." I said.

"I better let you go now so you can get ready, the show is about to start in a few." I could hear the crowd out there starting to assemble and the DJ was spinning all the latest hits. Sincere shook my hand and genuinely thank me for interviewing him before heading out to his awaiting fans. I could tell the exact moment he reached them by how high the octave level peaked in the next room over. I stayed behind a few extra minutes just so I could highlight and organize my notes then met back up with Chaz at the bar. The place was filled to the capacity. He and June appeared extremely busy as they multitasked taking orders and pouring mixed beverages. I wanted to help out so bad but I had my own commitment to fill.

"How did it go?" Chaz asked wiping his hands on a towel.

"Everything went well Sincere is very down to earth thank you for allowing me to conduct the interview here."

"No problem and you still going to mention the bar in the article right?" He asked.

"I got you Chaz my word is bond. I have nothing but good things to say about this place, its owner and patrons." I assured.

"I can guarantee after this article is published business here will never be the same, you're going to have to expand."

"Oh worrd, you thorough like that ma? That's what's up!"

"You'll see." I said with confidence.

"Yo Chaz, your sister just walked in." June hollered over the music. A look of relief washed over Chaz face.

"Bout time you got your ass here." He said changing up his expression as he grilled her.

"Shut up niggah I had to find a babysitter for Nahjir It aint my fault you can't control your jealous bitch." She shot back.

"I wasn't planning on working tonight." She slit her eyes at him with her hand on her rounded hip.

"D'Sire, this is my sister Nicole, Nicky this is the writer for Street Talk I was telling you about. She's interviewing the battle rappers tonight." Chaz said turning his attention on to me.

"Nice to meet you D'Sire." She rolled her eyes at her brother then smiled at me and extended her hand.

"I know you must think we crazy up in here. Especially with Tonya coming at you today. I told my brother to just let me straight rock that bitch but nooo he won't let me. She better be glad she got my nephew cause if she didn't I swear to God yo." She told me as she pounded her fist into her open hand. "That bitch would be a straight wrap; I can't stand her. I knew she was trying to trap my brother by getting pregnant because she aint nothing but a gold digging hoe." She emphasized hoe I glanced at Chaz he was busy on the other side of the bar helping June with a rowdy customer and wasn't paying attention to what was being said. I couldn't help but wonder how he would feel about his sister airing all his business though. Something told me that he was probably used to it. At first I couldn't tell because of the way they greeted each other but as Nicole talked on, it was evident that they were close and she was real protective over him even though he was older out of the two. Chaz narrowed his eyes in our direction.

"Girl take my number down maybe we can chill sometime. Let me go before I have to cuss my brother out in this bitch." She said sucking her teeth while writing it on a napkin. Chaz lifted the counter to let his sister behind the bar. Immediately they began to argue. It was comical because Nicole was every bit of five foot two at the most and Chaz was way over six feet and it was clear that she dominated. I made my way through the sea of party goers towards the back where the DJ booth and pool table where a certain familiar face caught my attention at first glance. It was Marcus the dude I met a few months back when T-Roy and I first started kicking it. He was playing pool with his boy Rick and looking a lil more built as he positioned himself over the oak Brunswick table. He appeared to be in deep concentration as the pool stick crashed hitting its mark knocking the number 6 red solid ball fluidly into the right corner pocket. Our eyes met. I scanned the perimeter in hopes of seeing Tyrell with no luck. Marcus leaned towards Rick, Rick nodded and glanced in my direction. I walked over and greeted the two.

"Hey you guys what's good?" I asked.

"Chillin, I'm here to support my mans Rick an them, they battle rapping tonight." Marcus said patting Rick on his shoulder.

"And I take it that you're covering the event." He added with assumption.

"Yes, as a matter of fact I am." I said holding up my camera.

"Can I get a couple of pictures of you two for the magazine? And rick I need to see you in the back for a few just to ask a couple of questions regarding the show later."

"No doubt I got you D'Sire." Rick said then sipped his Heineken.

"Congratulations on y'all single. It's been in steady rotation; every time I turn my radio on I hear it. Did y'all sign yet?"

"Naah we gonna remain independent for now until the right offer comes along and besides were more in control with what we want when it comes to our music."

"How's your man T-Roy doing? Is he coming tonight? We need to politic cause we bout to drop the single with his vocals next and we want to do some more work with him and we got a lawyer now so we more about our business." Rick said before hitting the eight ball with one clean stroke.

"Game." He gloated.

"Troy has been busy in the studio preparing for his next album so I haven't really been seeing much of him lately and I've been real busy myself with the magazine in all but when we do get up I'll let him know. Or maybe you should call him yourself."

"I thought about it but you just confirmed what I already knew anyways so I'll just wait for you to talk to him first and see what he says. I know how it is when you practically live in the studio and focused on your own project." Rick added with sincerity.

"Excuse me for a minute." I said walking towards the DJ Booth. DJ phenom handed me a manila folder with all the performer's government and stage names and a well written out line of what the event entailed. It was more than I expected and I was very grateful because it gave me a clearer vision for what I was to write. I took a few flicks of him. Then Chaz came over and helped so he and I could flick it up together.

"My bad D'Sire, I've been meaning to introduce you to everybody but I see you have no problem in getting acquainted." He said.

"I'm good Chaz I see how busy you are trust I don't have a problem introducing myself. If I did I wouldn't be in this field besides I know a few people in here so I'm alright."

"Ok but I just wanted to make sure you were straight that's all."

"Yo, Phenom you want something to drink?" Chaz yelled over the music.

"Yea let me get a Heineken."

"D'Sire, you want something to drink, eat?"

"No thank you Chaz I'm straight." I need all of tonight's contestants to come to the DJ Booth. We got D'Sire, representing Street Talk Magazine in the house tonight, and she wants to hear what you got to say." DJ Phenom said as he lowered the Locs song Renee'. A mob of people began to flow into the crowded room.

"I said contestants, contestants only." He shouted. The crowd didn't listen. I felt somebody grab my hand pulling me opposite of the congested frenzy that over spilled the area. If it hadn't been for my camera being strapped around my wrist I would have most certainly dropped it. I smiled at Tyrell not only because

He was my saving grace but because I've envisioned the moment we would meet again and masturbated on all the possibilities.

## CHAPTER 18

2000

"Oh my god nurse I just saw her finger move!" I faintly heard a woman's voice scream. I suddenly sensed a bunch of commotion in the room. I could hear several voices speaking at once, but could not make out what they were saying.

"You see there it goes again." I heard the woman cry out.

"D'Sire my name is Dr. Afmed." I heard him say in a thick Middle Eastern accent.

"If you can hear me please move your fingers again." I could hear him I was sure of it but I could not move them. It felt as if my fingers were being poked over and over again with a straight pin.

"I'm telling you I saw it move."

"Ma'am I'm not doubting what you saw but sometimes the nerve endings in a coma patient's body tend to spasm, giving off the effect of conscious movement." He explained.

"Ok folks lets clear the room." I heard the Dr. say. I could faintly hear the shuffling of feet as the people scrambled to leave.

"Oh father God please bring this child of yours out of this coma. Father God I ask you in the name of Jesus to heal her Lord, heal her sick broken body because I know you can make miracles happen. I ask that you release her spirit back to this Earthly plane so she can have a second chance at life and to see her beautiful baby girl grow up." This woman must be praying for someone else because I don't have a daughter. I thought to myself and floated back into the peaceful mist of the white light where I was safe. I stayed in a coma for over a year. Fifteen months to be exact. The only thing I remember was the crippling sense of fear that consumed my total being as I was sucked from my physical body through a dark vortex wind tunnel type thing into a soothing pure white light then a sudden reverse from the safe confines of the light back through the tunnel of fear followed by an excruciating thunder of pain in my head as I slowly blinked my eyes open. It was dark something was covering them. When I heard the sudden running of feet in the room I started to freak out because I did not know where I was and that something was terribly wrong. I felt an icy hand of someone restraining me as I kicked wildly and clawed at the tubes that ran down my throat. I felt a stinging sensation in my left arm as a warm liquid rode my veins like vampire venom instantly, transforming me into a slow moving, zombie until I could no longer fight but I had an acute sense of hearing and was totally aware of my surroundings. I remember a Dr. explaining to me that I was in a hospital and that my body suffered a great deal of trauma due to a gunshot wound to my head. He said I was lucky because the bullet lodged in my skull. Throughout the course of several days the staff of Yale Hospital gently explained to me a recap of the horrific event that nearly killed me. Mrs. Johnson the hospitals social worker told me that I was raped by my uncle and as a result I birthed a baby girl by cesarean. A blood test confirmed that my uncle was the father of the child. I also learned that my grandmother passed from a heart attack and that in the process of trying to take my life my uncle took his own, I broke down at that point and mourned my uncle's death.

I wanted nothing to do with the baby didn't even want to see her I went through several life altering weeks of mental and physical therapy. Dee Dee and Jamal were my only visitors and it wasn't hard to tell that they were an item now. That was cool with me she needed someone to turn to after Trent got killed during a robbery attempt and me being in a coma in all so I totally understood. They tried very hard to act normal around me but I saw right through them. I didn't think they meant any harm though. They probably just didn't know how to approach my situation. It's been three long months since the day I awoke from my death slumber. The doctors felt that I was mentally and physically strong enough to be discharged into the hands of the state because I had no family to take me in. I would have to live in an all-girls home until I was of legal age. On the very same day I left the hospital I signed closed adoption papers for a child my uncle and I conceived in hopes that she will never know her tainted past and be given the chance to live a normal life. Something that I knew I would never be able to provide for her. I had a very difficult time adjusting to my new living arrangements. There were eleven girls in the house including myself ranging from the ages of six to seventeen. They came from all types of backgrounds some of them been molested, witnessed the murder of their parents or just straight up out of control. We were all very different from one another yet shared one common conviction and that was that God hated us and the feeling was mutual. Our reasons varied mine were because he took my uncle away, the one person who truly loved me so much that he couldn't live without me. I still held my secret guarded although the others were very open in expressing their feelings and did so quite often then would wind up banging out because one threw the next one's business back with a twist of vengeance up in her face. I could remember one time in particular when shit hit the fan we were all watching love and basketball in the living room. Roslyn and Tonisha were at each other throats all day and the argument escalated into a full fledge first fight except Roslyn fought dirty. From out of nowhere she spit a razor blade into her hand slicing Tonisha's face, telephone cutting from ear to mouth in one swift motion Tonisha's skin separated exposing white meat and tendons. Unaware of being cut the fight continued into one great bloody mess Tonisha gained the upper hand slamming Roslyn's head into the wood table repeatedly until she was unconscious. Tonisha stood over Roslyn breathing hard looking straight like that bitch from the move Carrie during the bloody prom scene. Tonisha and Roslyn both left in an ambulance and when the police tried to question us we weren't fucking with them they couldn't determine who was at fault. We paid in other ways. The mother of the house, Mrs. Powell revoked what little privileges we did have for three months. It didn't faze me though because all I ever did was read books and write anyway. I became extremely consumed with any literature I could get my hands on and would become the main character in the story and get whisked away to other worlds. I became obsessed with rewriting the stories in my own words creating my own happy endings. My best work came through when the whole house in slumber. I would write for hours in the dark breaking night only to do it all again the next evening I was well reserved nobody fucked with me and I rocked alone. Mrs. Powell home schooled us so we would be protected, from the ridicule of other kids. Most of us at the house made front page headlines because the crimes committed against us including mines were so heinous. As an extra precaution she didn't allow newspaper inside the house or us to watch the news either. So it was strictly up to you if you wanted to air all your business to the house. Every time one of the girls would ask me I would just shut them out by saying that I didn't remember and it would work because all they did know was somebody shot me in the back of my head but they never knew who that somebody was and why. My hair was beginning to grow back in and pretty soon people who didn't know me would never be able to tell because all the scars from all the surgeries will be covered. Once a week a state appointed child psychiatrist would visit. We would all have to do a group session then she would see four of us separately for one on one. Her name was Dr. Martinez she was a pretty Puerto Rican woman very petite yet lacked emotion. I liked that about her no matter how horrible the subject at hand was she kept it stoned faced only an occasion scribble in her spiraled pad would indicate she was really paying attention. My one on one session always fell on the first and third Monday of every month. I dreaded them. "Hello, D'Sire." She said smiling as I entered, gesturing for me to have a seat. I plopped down on the green tweed tattered oversized chair.

"Hi, Mrs. Martinez." Her smile was not reciprocated.

"How have you been feeling?" She asked.

"Everything is still the same I feel fine."

"D'Sire, you give me the same answer every time we have a session. You mean to tell me nothing's changed in six months?" She asked with concern in her voice. "Nope still can't remember nothing, still don't feel nothing and still don't want to be sitting here right now." I said with a tinge of anger in my voice.

"Where would you rather be?" She asked crossing her leg under black, designer pencil skirt.

"Well the only place I rather be is somewhere where I know you can't help me get to so it doesn't make sense to tell you but besides there I rather be upstairs in my room reading a book or writing a story." I said crossing my arms over my chest and rolling my eyes.

"D'Sire, I may be able to help you, please tell me about the other place that you rather be." I sensed desperation in her voice.

"No I rather not talk about it. I have a headache. Now may I be excused?" Mrs. Martinez let out an aspirated sigh.

"D'Sire, would please bring some of your stories to our next one on one?"

"I'll think about it." I curtly said looking out the window.

"Ok then I will see you next time D'Sire have a good day." She said standing up. I walked out of the room and closed the door. I knew that Mrs. Martinez had a job to do and that was to get me to talk about my past with her.

And she longed for me to trust her enough to open up about all my secrets that I held about what me and my uncle did in the basement. I wasn't stupid but she was, for thinking I would ever tell her a damn thing. I wondered how Mrs. Martinez would feel if she knew how much I craved for my uncle's big dick how I fucked myself on a daily basis to the imagery of my uncles face and how I would do anything, I mean anything to bring him back. I was relieved to have the room to myself. I closed the door and curtains then undressed and slid into my bed. My pussy began to swell in anticipation of self-pleasure she was about to receive. I laid on my back and gently rolled my erect nipple in between my index finger and thumb and masturbated at the same time placing two fingers in and out my pussy and caressing my pulsing bud. My body spasmed and tears spilled from my eyes and cries of passion escaped my lips as I came over and over again to the vision of my uncle fucking me. Then drifted off to sleep where he waited in my dreams.

## CHAPTER 19

2003

"D'Sire, your cab is here Mrs. Powell yelled!" I could hear the cabbie beeping the horn like he aint have no sense. Today was the day I've been dreaming of since I stepped foot in this house. I was upstairs gathering up the last of my belongings which consisted of very few essentials and tons of books, pens and compositions which held three years of stories I've written. I was leaving, behind a pair of sneakers, three hoodies and a winter coat to accommodate these items.

"D'Sire!" Mrs. Powell voice was closer.

"Coming!" I yelled back. I took one last look at the room that held my secrets then headed down the stairs. I said goodbye to all my counterparts who lined up to see me off. Some of them were crying and even though I was touched I held my tears in tight.

"D'Sire I wish you well I know in my heart that you will make it. I knew since the day I first saw you lying in that hospital bed. I prayed for you every day. I know the good lord will protect you out there and I will continue to pray to make sure he does." Mrs. Powell said with sincerity. Her voice cracked as she spoke. She handed me an envelope.

"D'Sire, there is a few dollars and a phone number in here. Once you get settle into the woman's shelter I want you to call the number.

"The man's name is Mr. Bernstein he's waiting to hear from you ok."

"Who is he?" I questioned.

"Tell you the truth D'Sire I'm not sure but his phone number was in your file and I was told by the social worker to make sure that you received it upon discharge." Mrs. Powell hugged me tight and kissed me on my check. Tears streamed down her plump face and the lines around her eyes crinkled as she smiled at me.

"Now go head chile before your cab leave." She said over the cab's blaring horn.

"Thank you Mrs. Powell for everything." I said then headed out the door. The cool breeze of autumn air greeted me as colorful leaves danced circles in my path creating a colorful crunchy carpet under my feet. The cabby's scowl suddenly transformed into a huge smile once I approached. He was tripping over himself trying to help me with my bags. After placing my things in the trunk he just stood there staring at me. It made me feel weird so I cleared my throat out of nervousness.

"Ah yes yes I'm so sorry." He said as he fidgeted with back door handle to let me in. He sounded as if he was of African descent.

"My name is Re'mee." He said looking through the rearview I just stared out the window.

"What's a pretty young lady doing staying at a shelter? If I was your husband you would live in a big house with lots of babies to keep you busy and I would bring you all my money." He added I shivered at the thought avoiding eye contact. I could feel him staring at me I crossed my arms over my chest and held my elbows while I shifted in the seat. Air escaped the cracked worn grey leather from my weight. The cabbie continued to blabber on about his whole life story about escaping some war in Africa and how he ended up here going to school and driving cabs and the rest was blah blah blah as I tuned him out. I felt a headache slowly approaching. We passed a sign that said New Haven and drove on for about fifteen minutes before we finally reached our destination. I reached into the envelope Mrs. Powell gave me to pay him.

"No Ms. Beautiful I cannot accept money from you this ride was prepaid for by the state." He said smiling extra hard. He rushed out the cab to open my door and handed me a card with his name on it.

"Call me if you ever need a ride I will not charge you. Your beauty is payment enough." He said as he gathered my bags from the trunk. He left the engine running and walked me to the front door of the brick building.

"Thank you." I managed to say then he walked to his cab singing in his native tongue. He looked at me, smiled and finally pulled off. I looked up at the camera then pushed the doorbell. I squeezed my midsection not knowing what to expect. Once I heard the sound of footsteps approaching I took a deep breath and relaxed my body and convinced myself in my head that everything would be alright. It would always help me whenever I faced new challenges to compare myself to a book and make the situation a chapter. Whenever I did this I would vision in my mind the outcome that I wanted and it seemed to work for me like I possessed some type of sacred power or something.

An attractive dark skinned woman opened the door. "Hi I'm Barbara you must be D'Sire, come on in. Bill our new intake is here." She called down the hall. Bill, a tall medium build Caucasian man smiled at me and extended his hand. He then grabbed both my duffle bag and back packed and ushered me in. The couple led me to a small, cramped office that was only big enough to hold two desks and a file cabinet. Bill left out then returned with a grey metal fold up chair.

"Have a seat D'Sire I just need to get some information from you and tell you about the residence. We will then assign you a bed and locker for your things and give you a tour." He said as he donned his black framed reading glasses.

"Shall we begin?" Barbara left us alone and closed the door.

"D'Sire, I am the intake manager. My job is to oversee that residents here such as you are provided with the proper resources that fit your individual needs so that you could function productively through your transition back into society. This program is one of a kind here in CT it is only available to those whom suffered greatly as children due to traumatic experience and entered into adulthood with nowhere else to go. The men's side is around the back. I am here to help you. I understand that you may have some trust issues it is very common. I just hope that you will trust me enough so I can do my job." He sounded sincere, yet rehearsed. He must have said this same speech over a thousand times. I thought to myself.

"D'Sire, feel free to read the contract and the program rules then please initial acknowledging that you understand what you read, also you can sign your name at the bottom. If you have any questions by any means do not hesitate to ask." He said sliding a thick packet of paper to me. I sped read the whole thing and quickly initialed then signed my name. I pushed the packet back towards him. Bill hesitated a moment before picking up the papers. D'Sire, are you sure that you read and understand everything this packet entails? He asked with skepticism in his voice. In a matter of seconds, I was able to recite everything that I read almost verbatim plus explained to him what I felt it meant to me. At that moment Barbara entered the room to take me on a tour of the facility. We left Bill at his desk with his mouth wide open.

"Barbara don't I have to bring my bags?" I asked looking back at the office. "Yes we will bring them to you. First they have to be searched for weapons and drugs. Its precautionary we have to do it to every new intake to ensure the safety of our staff and residents. We also conduct random searches and urinalysis. In order to live here you must remain clean. This is zero tolerance program D'Sire." She added in more serious tone. Barbra led me down two flights of stairs into the basement.

"Here is our lovely kitchen." She said showcasing the appliances and opening cabinets and deep freezers.

"There is a resident cook who prepares all of the meals and on holidays we all join in." She said with a smile. In a room adjacent to the kitchen was the laundry room. It contained three coin operated washing machines with matching dryers and a long beige table for folding clothes. A small older Sony television sat mounted on a shelf on the wall. A cable box sat on top of it. The smell of soap powder and fabric softener lingered in the air. I inhaled deeply knowing that this was going to be my favorite place in the whole house. It seemed private enough for me to write my stories at and the atmosphere had a calming effect of some sort. I was definitely feeling it. Next she led me back upstairs through a long corridor. I could hear voices in the distance. The voices grew louder as we approached a large open room. Ten wooden bunk beds were lined up side by side. It didn't take me long to do the math that I would be sharing this space with nineteen other women. D'Sire, your bed is number 14-B. I glanced in the direction her eyes were settled on. Besides the obvious I was grateful to at least be a bottom bunk. The whole room fell silent as Barbara introduced me. It felt awkward to have so many people stare at me at one time. A couple women smiled a few of them grilled me and whispered to one another slitting their eyes. The energy in the room felt despondent very heavy. Barbara presence was met with phony ass hellos and counterfeit smiles she seemed oblivious to the resentment that lurked in the woman's hearts but I picked up on it immediately upon entering the room. D'Sire I'm going to leave you for a while so you could get settled in. There is clean linen in your locker. I'll be back shortly with your belongings. She said leaving the room.

"I bet you her eyes are fake you could tell she trying to be white." Someone said acidly.

"Fucking stank ass bitch. She better not even think about looking in Tyrone's direction I will straight rock her ass." Another said. I hear that girl you better keep an eye on that bitch I bet you she likes black men. She looks like the type."

"Yea I know I bet you she a fucking hoe, I aint worry about her she a straight up bum anyway look at her sneakers what the fuck kind are they?" She started cracking up.

"Yo, and her jeans. Who the fuck wears those anymore?" The other woman said. The two were rolling around slapping the bed laughing hysterically. I could hear others joining in on the conversation throwing in directs like razors slicing into my soul. After making my bed I laid in it with a sheet over my body. I turned and face the wall and fought hard against the tears as I lost the battle. They streamed my face in silence like perpendicular rain against a windshield as I tried so hard to block out the snide remarks that hammered my ears to no avail. I wondered to myself if these women knew my secrets and if they didn't, what else would make them say these things about me? There had to be a reason. I've must have done something to make them all hate me. I was jolted out of my thoughts by the disgusting sound of hog spit followed by the repulsive feeling of the sticky rancid smelling glob of phlegm that slowly slid down the side of my face. I leaped to my feet in rage.

"Who the fuck just spit on me?" I demanded. The whole room fell silent my heart quickened as I scanned the room. Still no answer, I nearly ran Barbara over as I bolted past her in the hallway towards the bathroom. I could hear her calling my name over the cackle of laughter as I slammed and locked the door cracking its wooden frame.

## CHAPTER 20

The first month I moved into the shelter was a living hell. I finally found out who the bitch was that spit on me, her name was Latoya she had a deep mocha complexion, full lips small breast and a huge ass that clapped every time she walked. She kept a different weave in her hair every week and wore all the latest fashion. She rocked with this other black chick named Renee'. Renee' had a dark complexion with big eyes thick frame and had a Rhianna type hair cut that was shaven on one side and dyed red and blond at the top. These two bitches were the ring leaders of all the chaos that went down. I also found out that they fuck with a couple of niggahs on the men's side Latoya's boyfriend name is Tyrone and Renee's is Maurice she also be fucking his boy Dre on the low. Tyrone and Maurice sell drugs and stay in the shelter just as a front and they spoil Latoya and Renee' with shopping sprees and lavish gifts that they keep stashed at a friend's house. I overheard these two girls by the name of Niecy and Michelle talking in the laundry room the other day while I was writing. Niecy was saying that Latoya was bragging about Tyrone buying her a condo and that she was moving in it in eight weeks and about the beautiful all white imported Italian leather living room set he took her to pick out at Masons.

"D'Sire, Bill would like to see you in his office please." Barbara said as I was trying to come up with the perfect ending to this murder mystery I was writing. She startled me. I was so deep in thought that I didn't hear her come up behind me. A feeling of nervousness crept into my chest as I entered Bill's office.

"Close the door, please have a seat." I sat down "My reason for calling you is because you have passed your thirty-day probationary period and you now qualify for a few extra privileges." He handed me a manila folder. "Go ahead look inside." I slowly opened it. The folder contained a seventy-five-dollar gift voucher to AJ Wright a clothing store in Hamden, a bus pass, and an application for a scholarship to Fairfield University's literature arts program I looked up at Bill. The gratitude I felt was overwhelming the bus pass was good for thirty days.

"We expect you to use it wisely. You may go out for six hours a day to seek employment." He added. "It is your responsibility to watch over these items because they will not be replaced if you lose them or if they get stolen. Understood?" I shook my head yes. "That's all and D'Sire, you should really consider sending in that application before the December 1st deadline I've read some of your work on the day you moved in here and you are indeed a natural." He said clearly unaware that he violated my privacy. Even though he did I still embraced his compliment.

"I'll think about it thank you Bill." I sincerely said. Then left the office. I had ulterior motives for what my six hours of freedom would be used for and it wasn't for job searching. I took the O bus downtown and sold the pass for twenty dollars and lucked out with thirty-five for the AJ Wright voucher. Then hopped the train to Bridgeport. As soon as I touched ground I dialed Dee Dee from a pay phone.

"Hello."

"Hi Dee Dee." I squealed.

"Oh my God D'Sire is that you?" She exclaimed. I could hear a baby in the background.

"Yes girl, I need you to come scoop me. I'm downtown at the train station."

"Ok I'll be right there don't go anywhere." We disconnected. I waited for about fifteen minutes. I heard a horn beep it was Dee Dee across the street and she was pushing an all-white big body 2003 Lexus. She waved excitedly from the car. Horns blared as I dodged traffic across the busy street. Dee Dee got out of the car and embraced me in a sisterly hug. I peeped movement in the back.

"Oh my god Dee is this you?"

"Yes girl that's Jamal Antwan Jr. She answered with a smile. Dee Dee's baby was adorable he was so chubby with a beautiful head of plump jet black curls. He babbled in his car seat kicking his legs.

"How old is he?"

"Just turned nine months on the sixteenth come on girl get in, it's cold our here." She said. We both hurried into the car.

"D'Sire look at you all grown up you are so pretty and I see you got your weight back up. Where you been? Me and Jamal called everywhere looking for you but no one would give us information because you were a minor. And I made sure my mother didn't change her phone number in hopes that you would call one day but you never did." She said as her eyes swelled with water.

"Dee I was in an all-girls group home for the past three years. The big raggedy brown house on Fairfield Ave we were restricted from using the phone and only came outside when new had to go at the doctor, dentist appointments and church."

"Oh my God D'Sire are you serious?"

"Yes Dee it was horrible but I adjusted and it didn't bother me no more. The mother of the house, Ms. Powell was a strict yet nice older woman who was very over protective of us because of all we've been through I further explained."

"Oh I see but what matters most is that you are here. It's crazy because I forgot Jamal Jr's teething medicine. She said I would have been devastated if I missed you call. Where are you staying at now?"

"I'm in a woman's shelter, on the Boulevard in New Haven; today was my first day out. They gave me a six-hour pass."

"Girl you don't have to stay in no shelter you could come stay with me and Jamal until you get on your feet." She offered I wanted so bad to say yes but declined.

"Thank you Dee but I'm going to stay in the shelter a lil while longer so I can receive all the benefits that I'm entitled to. They pose to help me get housing and whole bunch of other stuff."

"That's what's up then I don't blame you." besides I wouldn't feel comfortable living under the same roof with Jamal anyway but I kept that thought inside my head. Dee Dee lived on the North end of Bridgeport Chopsey hill Rd, Lake Forest area the house was beautiful surrounded by woods with a picturesque water view. The inside was breath taking with a grand spiraled staircase that descended from an open loft which contained the elegantly designed bedroom.

"Somebody hit the jack pot." I said kiddingly.

"Yea girl, Jamal's mother passed last year and since he was her only child he inherited it. It's a shame though she never got a chance to meet the baby she was such a sweet woman." Little Jamal was knocked out from the ride Dee Dee carefully took his coat off then placed him on his stomach in the plush baby blue sleep –n- play in the living room.

"Dee besides the obvious of missing you like crazy I came because I need your help." I stated.

"Sure D'Sire, whatever you need, what's wrong?" She asked with a look of concern.

"For starters I need clothes, I was hoping that you had a few things lying around that you're not wearing anymore." I said looking at the floor.

"That's it? Girl you had me over her bout to have a whole heart attack." She grabbed my hand and I tripped over a couple of stairs trying to keep up with her. She opened the door to her walk in closet and started pulling articles of designer clothes with tags off their hangers and piling them up in my arms until I couldn't carry no more. Next we raided her shoe collection she piled at least twenty pairs of various designer shoes in boxes that stacked over my head.

"Dee Dee slow down I can walk into the shelter with all this stuff. Its mad suspect." I explained the whole procedure. I took three outfits and one pair of boots. Dee Dee would have to bring the rest of the clothes in a little at a time. The shelter didn't have a limit on what we could have. Everything was considered a donation no matter where it came from. Dee Dee and I spent the rest of our time catching up on the past few years and I told her about the problems I was having at the shelter with Latoya and Renee'. She made me laugh when she demonstrated how she would wupp they ass. She also took me to the hair store and bought me a gold n hot ceramic flat iron and all the necessities to keep my hair up. Dee Dee drove me back to New Haven.

"Here D'Sire, take this and make sure you keep it on you I don't want to have to come up here and beat a bitch down for robbing you." she said trying to look hard. I gave her a hug.

"Thank you Dee, I love you girl." I said tucking the 900 hundred dollars in my bra.

"I love you D'Sire I'll be back up on Sunday to drop some more stuff off to you k."

"Ok Dee I'll see you later." I said and watched my best friend drive off. I made it back seven minutes' shy of my allotted six hours. After signing in I headed to the bunkroom in an attempt to stash my loot but was intercepted by the hateful glares of Latoya and her nemesis Renee. Out of nervousness I fumble with the combination of my locker. A surge relief escaped as I felt the release along with the golden click like music to my ears as I took the articles of clothing from the bag, folding before neatly placing them in their prospective places. Next I placed all my cosmetics and hair care products on the shelf. The shoe box that contained my gently used black Louis Vuitton boots found a resting place on the floor. I smiled inward as the feeling of joy began to climb back into my system. I was determined not to let Latoya ruin my day. I knew now that I've done nothing wrong and the hate that reeked from her pours was fueled by jealously towards me. I was fully aware of how her boyfriend Tyrone watched me behind his dark designer shades and she was too she knew that it would be only a matter of time before he would succumb to his weakness. I grabbed my composition book pencils and two erasers before securing my locker. I ignored Latoya's snide remarks as I headed towards the basement stairs. The last thing I remember was the feeling of being pushed followed by a loud crunch and very cold as my legs went numb, and the sound of laughter from the top of the stairs. I made a full recovery. The doctor said that I was very lucky to have landed the way I did and that the tiny hip fracture could have been worse. 9 days later I was discharged from the hospital. I kept a tight lip on the events that led to my so called accident careful not to tell nobody not even Dee Dee. It was no surprise to come back to find out that my locker was broken into my clothes were bleached. Boots along with cosmetics and hair products stolen and the worst that could ever happen, all my stories that I've ever written for the past three years were strewn throughout the locker in a watery grave of torn confetti. I ignored the pain as I fell to my knees and mourned the last of what was left of my soul.

## CHAPTER 21

Oh revenge, it's so beautiful, it radiates like sparks of light that dance from a flawless diamond as the sun hits it, especially when the one you seek it on has no clue what is in store for them. From a payphone I dialed the upscale furniture store that was to deliver Latoya's living room set.

"Masons where living it up has no boundary this is Amy speaking how may I direct your call?" A pleasant speaking sales associate chimed through the phone.

"Ah yes my name is Latoya Stevens, I am calling to confirm that the furniture my boyfriend bought will be sent to the correct address." I said in my most pleasant disguised voice that spoke money.

"Oh yes Ms Stevens I remember you. I'm the one who helped you pick out the beautiful set." I began to panic.

"The address Mr. Williams has down according to the computer says 1201 Rosedale lane number 42-A Hamden, CT is that correct?" She inquired.

"Yes as a matter of fact it is." I beamed from the other end.

"Thank you Amy."

"Ms Stevens."

"Yes." I froze.

"Have a lovely day and please send my regards to Mr. Williams. Oh and delivery is still set for wed Dec 15th will the key still be under the mat?"

"Yes it will and you have a great day as well." A satanic grin crept across my lips as I hung up the receiver. December 15th was more than two weeks away so that gave me plenty of time to devise and execute my plan. Dee came through with ten times the amount of designer, clothes, shoes and accessories than what was stolen from me along with enough pens, pencils and composition books to fill a classroom. She and Jamal would visit twice a week with gifts in tow. I passed on my goodwill to people in the house who were less fortunate than me. Latoya and Renee were no longer the center of attention and their hatred for me was evident. While cleaning the area under my bed I notice a wad of crumbled paper. Using the broom handle I retrieved it. I was about to toss it but there was something oddly familiar about it. Grey dust bunnies hopped from their crinkled confines as I flatted the ball out. It was the application for Fairfield University. I took it as a sign from the universe. I placed the paper in between a pillow case then grabbed the iron out of the linen closet. Next I placed the iron on its lowest setting then proceeded to run it across the fabric carefully so I wouldn't burn it. The application felt warm to the touch almost good as new except for a couple of creases. I read it thoroughly then completed it. I spent the rest of the day composing one fictitious story of 500 words as required, no less. Tomorrow was

December first and I was determined to make sure that these two papers made it to the college by any means necessary. The next morning dawned a pearl grey and the sheeting rain smacking against the window is what woke me from my slumber. My body felt heavy as I lugged myself out of the twin size bunk. The clock inside my locker read 5:29 am. It was way too early for me but I had a mission to accomplish so I gathered all of my hygiene essentials, secured my locker and made way to the bathroom to take care of my business. The shower was refreshing and the Victoria secret pear glace shower gel that Dee Dee bought me awoke my senses as I envisioned myself in the bathroom of a luxury sky rise in Manhattan overlooking the Hudson just Like in a book I read about when I was in the group home. I remembered placing me as the main character the owner of a successful public relations firm in New York and rewriting the whole entire story it only took me a month to recreate the whole book the title was of it was, My Time to Shine. Bout time I was ready to head out the door it was already at 7:30 am I grabbed my tan London fog full length rain coat along with the oversize Fendi monogrammed umbrella Dee Dee gave me and with papers safely tucked away, I signed out and rushed into the raging storm determined, while the rest of the city slept their dreams away. I waited at the bus stop for what seemed well beyond an hour and with each passing minute I was feeling as though this was a bad omen contrary to what I thought yesterday. I felt dejected as thunder crashed and lightning struck something in the near distance confirming my fears. I spent all the money that Dee Dee given me on bull shit and I was now regretting it. The rain drops assaulted my face blinding me even from under the protection of my umbrella. A swerving yellow cab almost ran me down splashing muddy cold rain water all over me as I made an unsuccessful attempt to step down from the curb. The unruly cabbie blared his horn, causing me to jump back just in time. My curses went unheard as the howling wind carried them into the opposite direction. Suddenly a thought came to mind. Careful this time I crossed the street to the pay phone and dialed all sevens.

"Cab," a nonchalant dispatcher answered on the other end.

"Hi I need Re'mee to pick me up."

"Lady, who the hell is Re'mee? I have over sixty cabs out there, what's the cab number?" He blared.

"I just called the cab number." I protested.

"No, the number on the side of the cab."

"Hold on please." I said in a desperate tone and closed my eyes.

"Look lady I aint got all day time is money." He barked. Something in my visual came up it looked like the number 20.

"Number 20." I blurted.

"Where are you?"

"At the corner of Ella T Grasso Boulevard and Washington." I replied. The irate dispatcher rudely hung up on me without a goodbye. About 45 minutes past and through my obscured vision I could see a blurry blob of yellow slowly approaching I still could not tell if that was him from where I was standing. The brakes screeched as the cabbie pulled up to the curb and came to a complete stop. The automatic window whirled down and I slowly lifted my head and let out an emotional audible gasp as I looked into the smiling eyes of Re'mee my saving grace.

"Oh god beautiful it's you, get in." he ushered frantically. My body actually burned as my temperature adjusted.

"What on God's green earth are you doing out in this nasty weather?" My teeth chattered as I tried to explain my application, the deadline and thanking him all at the same time. It wound up coming out in one big rambling mess. I took out the application and pointed.

"Ok, so you need to go to Fairfield University correct? I nodded my head yes.

"No problem." He got on his radio.

"Car 20 to dispatch."

"Go car 20."

"Unavailable till further notice."

"Roger that car 20." Re'mee turned off the meter then pulled off into the slow crawl of traffic. We finally made it in an hour for a trip that would normally take only around twenty-five minutes, due to a six car pileup on the highway. As soon as we passed the mangled mess, traffic eased up a bit. I was able to talk now and I graciously thanked Re'mee for the look out and offered to pay him back every dime he missed out on but he declined. This is my way of giving back to God he proudly stated as we rolled to a stop of the scenic campus. My silent protest to the universe was answered as Re'mee offered to wait for me. There was only one lone car in the parking lot. I hurried to the double doors and my heart leaped out of my chest when I read. All classes cancelled due to storm.

"No this can't be!" I said out loud while yanking the door handle. To my surprise it flew open with ease. I looked back at Re'mee. He was bobbing his head to music. Once inside the massive school I had no idea where to go. The rubber bottom of my boots squeaked as I took each step on the shiny tiled floor echoing throughout the hall. Every time I would stop at a door an eerie silence fell causing my senses to heighten. I took the stairs to the second floor. To my left there was a door about ten feet away that said science lab. Something within me compelled me to enter the slightly jarred door. A janitor's bucket that smelled of wax was the first thing I spotted once I slipped inside. The room was dimly lit and set up just like the lab on CSI. Professional microscopes, Petri dishes and test tubes were neatly lined up at each station. A huge chart of the compound elements adorned the wall along with portraits of the great Einstein and Isaac Newton in black in white. There was a metal container on the counter with a warning label on it. I picked it up and read. WARNING: Acid if not properly handled can cause death or other serious conditions. Without thought I slipped the container in my coat pocket. The sound of whistling startled me as I hid behind what appeared to be the teacher's desk. It was the janitor coming to retrieve his mop bucket. He turned off the lights and whistled his way out the door. I inhaled a deep sigh of relief knowing how close I was to being caught and hurried my ass out of the class room. I gently closed the door and wiped off the handle then headed opposite of the direction the janitor left. Finally, after getting lost in what seemed like one big circle I finally found the administrative office. There was a stack of applications just like mine on the desk I didn't even think about ringing the bell for assistance I just placed my application with attached story on the top of the pile and hauled ass out the building and into the cab that patiently waited. Our trip back was quicker north bound on the highway partially because people were heeding Governor Rowland's warning about not being on the roads due to weather conditions so I made It back to the shelter before my pass ran out. I kissed Re'mee on the check and thanked him again as I took his card this time promising not to lose it. After signing back in and getting chewed out by staff for leaving out in this weather and so on I managed to make it to the bunk room. I peeled off my cold wet clothes that stuck to my body like second skin, took a quick hot shower then slipped into a pair of Juicy Couture flannel pajama bottoms and oversized Gap sweat shirt. I gathered all my wet clothes in a plastic laundry basket and headed downstairs to dry them. Thankfully the laundry room was empty.

The washing machines and dryers were usually rigged and this time was no different so I just threw everything inside and turned the knob to high heat then made a cup of hot chocolate in the kitchen. I sat at the table sipping and thinking about the third step to my plan that seemed to be magically coming together all on its own. The storm finally passed. After three days of torrential rain, that shut the city down and having to deal with Latoya and Renee I needed to get out. The sun was determined to make its presence know from behind the clouds with an occasional beam here and there today. I bundled up in Guess jeans, a black Abercrombie hooded sweater and black genuine fur Oscar ski boots, I snapped the buckle on my North Face and bolted out of the door into the icy streets of New Haven, destination public library. I needed access to a typewriter so I could compose a letter that could not be traced. This time the bus arrived on schedule. It was so crowded that I had to stand and hold on to the overhead bar to keep balance. Two bums argued in the next row over. They held the bus hostage with the assault of deadly breath and funk.

"Niggah, I'm telling you right now if you don't find a way to get another bottle I'm a bust a cap in yo ass."

"With what? Yo looks. I told you niggah somebody must of stole it."

"Aint nobody stole the Night Train Freddy; I know you got the shit stashed somewhere!"

"I aint got it and since you don't wanna believe me we could go our separate ways Thomas." I tuned the rest of the conversation out while trying desperately to hold my breath. Finally, several stops later we arrived downtown. I swallowed several gulps of fresh icy air in an attempt of ridding my lungs of the contamination they've been exposed to due to Thomas and Freddy's toxic conversation. I quickly made my way across the green into the massive building which was sacred ground as far as I was concerned. The library for me is what church is to religious people, it deserves the upmost respect. Some days I would come just to get away from the daily chaos of the shelter and use up my whole six-hour pass as I became one with the books. Today was different though I was on a mission. I could not allow the distraction of what I loved the most deter me from what needed to be done. Just as I knew it would be the typewriter sat in the empty room alone waiting for me as if it knew I had a secret to tell. I fed it a piece of plain white fax paper and began to strike the keys. Dear Latoya I just want you to know that you mean the world to me. Do not tell nobody about this letter not even Renee' if you do I will find out. I have a surprise for you, meet me at the condo at 6:30 pm sharp on December 13th don't call me don't ask no questions I love you and wear something sexy.

## CHAPTER 22

Present

After the show I conducted the rest of my interview and flicked it up with all the contestants and party goers. I thanked everybody and promised to keep in touch. Once the magazine published the article everyone interviewed would receive their own personal copy. Tyrell stayed behind to help me with my things.

"D'Sire, you want to get something to eat? We could go to a diner or something."

"How about Denny's that's on the way home for both of us." I said

"That's what's up I could use me some Denny's steak and eggs scrambled with cheese right about now." Tyrell said lifting his shirt exposing a well-defined six pack. Pretending not to notice, I popped the trunk and placed my briefcase inside. Damn this niggah look good I thought to myself but I would have sworn he heard by the way he eyed me.

"What?" I asked innocently.

"What you thinking about D'Sire?"

"Nothing but how hungry I am." I said lying through my teeth.

"You ready?" I asked getting into my car.

"Yea, I'll follow you." He said deactivating the alarm to his midnight blue costumed painted Lincoln Navigator. Butter Love by Next blared through the Infinity sound system catching me off guard seconds after he turned the truck on. I pulled up on the side of him.

"What do you know about that?" I asked.

"More than you think." he said, switching up to Jagged Edge, Gotta Be.

"OH shit this is my song." I said singing off key but not caring.

"Is that a mix cd?" I asked.

"Yea, I made it myself. If you want, I'll burn you a copy it got all the cuts on it." He offered before I could ask.

"Ooo I can't wait. I can only imagine what you go up there." People were spilling out of the club.

"Aight lets slide before we get stuck in this parking lot." I said then pulled off. The food at Denny's was always blazing. I ordered the same thing as Tyrell. The only difference was that I could not eat my whole meal. I asked for a doggie bag. I was definitely going to reheat it in the morning. Aint no shame in my game.

"Tyrell, I'm going to be up for a while piecing this article together I could use the company. Do you want to come through for a minute?" I caught myself asking. Oh god I hope I don't sound desperate. I thought to myself I had no business inviting this man to my crib two something in the morning.

"Sure." He said sounding surprise Tyrell followed me to my condo and parked his truck in the guest spot next to my car. We headed up the elevator making small talk. I kicked off my heels and asked Tyrell to do the same he obliged.

"Would you like a drink?" I asked as he took the scene in.

"Yea what do you have?"

"Everything the bar has." I answered. I poured Tyrell's drink and left the whole gallon out so he could help himself. I made myself an Alize' with cranberry juice.

"I'm having a party Friday would you like to come? You can invite a few heads if you like."

"Word? Ok that's what's up I'm definitely in the building." His enchanting smile adorned his face. I excused myself and threw on a pair of sweat pants and a blue tee shirt that said Yale University on it, and pulled my hair back in a ponytail.

"You got a nice ass crib D'Sire."

"Thank you." I opened the patio door. Tyrell stepped onto the balcony.

"Damn girl I'm on top of the world." He said with his arms spread out doing a poor imitation of Tony Montana from Scarface. I just shook my head and laugh.

"Ok Tony I got work to do." I said grabbing my laptop then pouring myself another drink. The alcohol was starting to take effect but I knew that I had stay focused on my assignment or my boss was going to kill me. I tuned the stereo in to Hot 93.7, late night love. Linda Reynold's sultry voice melted me like butter as she introduced Escape's hit song 'My little Secret'. Tyrell sat on the floor next to me and watched as I hammered ferociously at the keyboard.

"D'Sire."

"Huhh?"

"What's up with you and T-Roy."

"What about us?" I asked without looking.

"Do you two still fuck around?" He asked more specific.

"Yea we fuck around but we don't go together if that's what you really want to know." I said still typing.

"Oh so you a free agent?"

"Yes Tyrell I'm single."

"So your boy wouldn't mind if I did this and this." He said kissing the side of my neck. I closed my eyes. Tyrell's lips against my skin felt so good, and the wetness between my thighs expressed interest as well. I closed my laptop and gently kicked it out the way as I titled my head back granting Tyrell the permission he waited for to explore the rest of my body. He pulled my tee shirt over my head and hungrily took my breast into his mouth next he slid my sweat pants off and gently kissed my stomach all the way down my thighs. My body squirmed as my pussy came alive begging for equal treatment. Tyrell paid attention to detail because next thing I knew my panties were off and his tongue and my clit were dancing and I was screaming in ecstasy. He literally made eating pussy into an art form. I unbuckled his Louis Vuitton belt and Tyrell kicked off his jeans. He reached into his pocket and took out a gold foiled Magnum rubber and handed it to me I yanked off his boxers and took his huge dick into my hands and slid the condom on. He then picked me up and carried me to the patio, and I wrapped my legs tightly around his back as he gripped my ass and carefully inched his anaconda into me and rode me up the wall straight into ecstasy.

## CHAPTER 23

It was August 14 the day of my party. Angel my party planner and now Sasha have been handling all the intricate details so all I had to do was focus on doing me, which meant day at the spa. It's been a while since I saw T-Roy because I had to cancel on him due to my early morning rendezvous with Tyrell. I blamed it on the article which was only a partial lie because it really did have to be finished before the 5 am deadline. Tranquility Day Spa exceeded my expectations. The staff went above and beyond when it came to making me feel relaxed for my special day you would have thought it was my wedding day by the treatment I received. The spa came highly recommended by Sasha, and now I see why he frequents on a regular basis. It's so much pricier than the one I go to but it is well worth it. I even paid extra to become a member. My cell phone was on silent the whole hour and 45 minutes I was in heaven. I had 13 missed calls several texts and two e-mail blast from Monica. From my car, I returned the important calls. The texts would just have to wait until I got home I didn't need the distraction while I drove. As I continued to scroll through the phone a call came through Jazzlyn's name blinked on the screen.

"Hello?" I pushed the speaker.

"Hi D'Sire, I was just calling to ask if you needed help with anything."

"Thanks Jazz I appreciate the offer but everything been taken care of already. Where are you at anyway?" I could hear horns blaring in the back ground.

"In traffic still in the city but it's starting to ease up now. I should be in CT in about an hour." She said.

"Ok, that's what's up. Are you coming straight to my crib or did you have other plans?"

"Dominick doesn't have to be at the hospital until around 9:00 tonight, so I'm going to play catch up with him for a while then shower and change over there that's unless he is paged to go in sooner."

"Oh, ok I understand his hectic schedule if anything changes you can always get dressed over here. It's too bad he can't make it through." I added.

"Oh well, girl I'm still have me a good time. Didn't you say T-Roy was bringing some of his boys?"

"Yea girl some industry niggahs." I said.

"Shit I'm kind of glad Dominick's ass can't make it. I might get lucky tonight. Hold on D'Sire I got another call."

"D'Sire, we done spoke him up, this is Dominick girl I'll hit you back when I get down there."

"Ok Jazz I'll be around drive safe."

"You too bye." We disconnected. I still had some time to kill so I decided to hit up my favorite Dominican spot to get my hair done. It was Friday so I already knew it was going to be an all-day affair. Just as I figured, the parking lot was full to the capacity so I had to park my car on the narrow side street and hope my ride was in one piece when I returned. Meehas Bonita was located on Ferry Street, the Fair Haven section of town. Most of the residents were of Latin decent it was a close nit community and the people seemed content despite of the impoverish conditions they were subjected to on a daily basis. Over all this was the best spot to get a dubbie and I took my chances on a biweekly basis of my car getting broken into all in the sake of beauty and the special homemade conditioner Olga the shop's owner put in my hair. The first time I tried it I was hooked. Evidently so is everyone else in the city because her place stays packed and no matter how much money I offer, she aint giving up the recipe. If she knew any better she would mass market that shit.

"Hola D'Sire." The dark skinned thick Dominican chick said as I entered, it was Olga's 18-year-old daughter Lucreesha who also worked at the shop. Her hair was up in a dubbie wrap secured with several black bobby pins and she had on a tight pair of cheap but cute skinny jeans, a black tee shirt that said baby girl and some pink fuzzy house slippers. Lucressha was very pretty with a nice body and she knew it too. She stayed in the mirror more than her client's hair.

"Hola Lucreesha. Is your mom here today?" {Please say yes}

"Si she's in the back rinsing out color." She said with a thick accent but I understood.

"How long is the wait?" I asked bracing myself for the answer.

"Thirty meenuts." She untruthfully stated. I looked at the sea of chicks waiting for their turn in the chair and their dissatisfaction from the long wait was evident. Julia and Francis were Olga's other daughters Julia was 14 and 9 months pregnant. Frances was 16 and only washed hair so technically it was only three of them I did the math. My wait time was approximately three hours unless I get lucky and a few people walk out. I grabbed a Black Hair magazine and water out of the vending machine and took a seat next to a woman who was rocking a crying baby and mentally prepared myself for the long ass wait. My cell phone vibrated, it was Sasha.

"Girl we are almost done, can't wait to see your face when you walk in. Where you at anyway? You been gone all day."

"I'm at Meehas Bonita."

"Oh lord D'Sire I don't know why you keep giving those illegal bitches your money."

"But, they're the best." I wined.

"Yea whatever I'll see you tomorrow when you get here. I guess I'll have to fill in as hostess tonight. Fuckin with that raggedy ass shop on a Friday you'll never make it to your own party."

"Two chicks already walked out so."

"Whatever trick, Angel and I are about to take a break if you know what I mean."

"You and Angel just better not be taking it in my bed."

"Here he comes got to go. D'Sire by the way your condo is off the chain ciao." I swear to god if Sasha and Angel fuck in my bed I'm going to seriously hurt them both. Suddenly I felt anxious to get home as I began to imagine the two of them in various compromising positions. Finally after two hours of self-torture my name was called and when I stepped out of the shop looking like Pocahontas all the time it took was well worth it. When I stepped into my crib it took me a moment to realize where I was. I stood in the doorway with my mouth hanging open and my eyes wide as I took in the enchanting scene that displayed itself before me. A flash snapped me back to earth. It was Sasha bitch ass capturing my facial expression with his Sony digital camera.

"Sasha, I swear on everything I love you better erase that picture!" I yelled reaching for the camera.

"See Angel I told you she would love it Sasha squealed looking at the picture.

"Ooh this is my new screen saver I'm about to forward it to everybody on my call list." He teased.

"Oh Sasha hush now I want to hear from D'Sire." Sasha sucked his teeth.

"Yea, you two definitely out did yourselves." The turquoise silver and white color scheme looked magical. I originally picked those three colors because they were unisex but now that I actually see them in my living space they seem very soothing to the eye, tranquil like. Hundreds of helium filled balloons looked like blue sky and clouds with silver lining as they swayed to a silent peaceful rhythm atop my cathedral ceiling. Spiraled glittered ribbon danced from them lending the illusion of mystery. Everything was beautiful from the sheer fabric draped over the windows to the pillows on my couch. Votive candles were everywhere and the mirrored bar was stocked over the capacity. The generous buffet was stored in several coolers and the refrigerator. Angel said he would set up the tables a half hour before the guest was to arrive. The outside patio was decorated as well. Clear star lights hung over head. I couldn't wait until night fell to see the full effect. My money was definitely well spent and for all of this I would have not had a problem with spending double. I knew that Angel went above and beyond than what he was mandated. I wrote him a generous check for his services and promised him a good deal if he wanted ad space in the magazine to promote his business in the future.

"Thanks D'Sire I will be glad to take you up on the offer." He said smiling.

"Well hun, I have to scurry off for a couple hours, Angel and I have to get ultra-glammed for tonight." Sasha said giving air smooches.

"Ok thanks again you guys, I have to get ready myself I'll see you later." My dress was hot to death it was an Alexander McQueen original. All black lace one shoulder piece that rode perfect on my thick thighs. I found a cute pair of Christian Louboutin red bottom snake skin stilettos to set it off. I've must have tried the outfit on at least five times prior to this day but something about the way my skin glowed against the fabric of the dress just seemed more vibrant to me. I took it back off and laid it on the bed and wrapped myself in a bath towel. Lonely Starr blasted through my phone. It was T-Roy.

"Hello."

"Hey baby what's it looking like?"

"Everything is good but I could tell you what would be even better." I said.

"What's that?"

"You, me and a pre party performance."

"Then buzz me in I'm right outside."

"Oh my god Troy, why didn't you call first?"

"Because I wanted to surprise my baby. You going to let me in or what?" I ran to the intercom system. His white Benz filled the security screen. I buzzed Troy in then ran to my bedroom to fix myself up. I threw on a wife beater and a pair of black BeBe boy shorts, the ones with the Swarovski crystal letters on the butt, his favorite and I fixed my hair. It's been a minute since I've seen him and I wanted to make a good impression being that he caught me off guard in my element and all. A few short minutes later I heard a light tap at the front door. Troy looked so handsome even in his regular street clothes. He had a Louis Vuitton overnight bag in one hand and a garment bag that said Versace hung over his shoulder. As soon as he stepped in the door I jumped on him. He dropped his bags on the floor just in time to catch me and he kicked the door closed behind him. T-Roy gripped my ass squeezing it as he carried me to the bedroom kissing me. He gently laid me on my back and slid the boy shorts off. I damned there ripped the wife beater to shreds trying to get out of it. T-Roy was much smoother than me in that department. He let out a sexy chuckle and helped me out of what was left of it. He then planted soft kisses slowly all over the front of my body starting from my closed eyelids all the way down to my toes next he turned me on my stomach and my body shivered into over drive as he repeated the whole process all over again this time to the back leaving no spot untouched, and my senses were heightened from the relaxed state my body was in due to all the pampering it received today but god damnnn. Tranquility Day Spa aint got shit on this niggah he was really working them lips and tongue.

"Ooh baby yes right there." I whispered as he started eating my pussy from behind I was on all fours now going crazy.

Every time he drove his tongue in deep he would spread my ass. Next T-Roy somehow on some acrobatic shit maneuvered himself under me. He was now on his back, his face was directly in my pussy and he had his arms wrapped around my thighs sucking the life out my shit.

"Oh my god Troy, I'm cumin. I'm cuming baby!" I screamed without shame. Troy slid from under me like a mechanic does when he's working under a car. He kicked his jeans and boxers off and unlike me gracefully came up out of his shirt. I straddled T-Roy and guided his erect Mandingo into the fat folds of my dripping pussy.

"Oh my god baby I miss this ass so much, yess D'Sire ride daddy dick D'Sire, ride it baby." Something about those familiar words made me go buck wild on that niggah dick. I rode it as if my life needed it to sustain. The controlled rhythm of my inner muscles had that niggah screaming my name. T-Roy sucked on my titties as they bounced in his face. I begged him to suck them harder as I fucked him faster in a squatted position while rotating my hips. I could feel Troy legs stiffen. He squeezed his eyes tight as he shouted out my name busting his hot seed into me and I quickly followed suite creaming all over his dick. We shared silence for a moment, catching our breath. T-Roy kissed my forehead.

"I missed you baby, How did the interview go?"

"Everything went well Sincere is very humble and I enjoyed talking to him he's not cocky like most mainstream artists. Did you know that his real name is Sincere?"

"Nawww I didn't know that, I'm glad it went well."

"Oh and I put in a good word for you too, he told me he will call."

"That's what's up my lil niggahs Tyrell and em called. He said that you invited them to the party, when did you bump into him?" My heart beat intensified. I had a feeling that T-Roy already knew but was trying to see if our stories were consistent.

"Um he was at the event, his boy Rick was battling some dude Rhino, Rhino won though." I added in hopes of ending the conversation.

"What did yall do after that?"

"Nothing, why is there a problem?"

"Nawww, but it's cool that you invited him."

"Yea I told him that he could bring whoever he wanted."

"That was nice of you."

"Troy."

"Yes bae."

"I have a surprise for you." I said as I disappeared from the room. I returned with a manila folder and handed it to him.

"What's this?" He asked.

"If I tell you then it won't be a surprise, now go ahead and open it." He placed the folder in his lap and began to examine its contents. T-Roy smiled then began to read the proposal for his restaurant Oblivion out loud.

"Thank you bae." He said hugging me tight.

"This means so much to me. When did you have the time to do all of this plus plan your party?"

"It wasn't hard, I had a chance to work on it at the office and researched everything from my computer." I didn't plan on giving him the proposal just yet because there were a few things that needed to be added and I couldn't help but to smile inward because it ceased the conversation about Tyrell for now. T-Roy and I fucked for about an hour from my bedroom to the shower. We both threw on comfortable clothes because we still had about three hours to kill before the guest were to arrive. Angel and Sasha arrived together, an hour before the party was to begin to put the finishing touches, which added more splendor to the already lavish decor. They looked equally handsome. Angel had on white Georgio Armani slacks with a light purple dress shirt, a beige designer belt and Ralph Lauren camel hide sandals Sasha appeared more casual. He wore faded light denim semi fitted Express jeans, Baby blue Ralph Lauren Polo shirt with white on white Jean Paul Gaultier canvas sneakers that must of cost a fortune because of the name. His stainless steel and diamond leather strap Louis Vuitton time piece was gorgeous.

"Ms. D'Sire, why aren't you dressed yet?" Asked Sasha as he raised a perfectly arched eyebrow. I'm about to get dressed Sash,

Troy and I were talking and lost track of time." I answered in defense of my attire.

"Umm hum. You hear this little lying heifer hun?" Sasha said to Angel but was looking at me. Bitch, I can tell by your lopsided wrap that you and Mr. T-Roy were doing way more than talking." He added.

"Sasha shhh, he's in my bedroom."

"Oh my bad, tell him to come out, me and Angel want to meet him."

"Calm down he's getting dressed. He'll be out in a few. Make yourself a drink, better yet why don't you go help Angel set up the buffet."

"Oh no I know you aint trying to put me to work. Angel hun do you hear this trick?"

"Sasha please." I begged in whisper form.

"Ok, since you did say the magic word. Angel would you like a drink?"

"Sure, I'll take an Alize' with a splash of hypnotic and a twist of lime on the rocks please. Sasha, Angel I want to take your picture." I grabbed my digital camera off the counter.

"Ready, one two three click. Ooo yall look so cute together." I said showing them. They smiled at each other as they admired the picture. Troy finally emerged from my bedroom looking like the cover of a GQ magazine. Sasha almost dropped my camera. He had on black Versace dress pants with a matching

Lycra infused fitted shirt that showed off his impeccable physic, black Stacy Adams alligator shoes with a black alligator belt. He rocked a platinum Cuban link chain with a flooded out diamond cross, his pinky ring was iced out and two large flawless diamond dripped from his ears T-Roy looked hot to deff.

"Hi I'm Troy." T-Roy extended his hand out.

"And you are?"

"I'm Sasha I mean Saul and this is my friend Angel."

"Hi Troy nice to meet you." Angel said.

"So you two are the ones responsible for this beautiful transformation being displayed in my baby's condo." Troy said flashing his million-watt smile melting both Sasha and Angel.

"Do you have a card? I might need some interior decorating done to my crib pretty soon and I probably could get you some clients." He added.

"I don't have any business cards but you can take my number?" Angel said clearly flattered.

I turned on my system and Sonny Seagram's, a local rapper from Bridgeport; mix tape cd began to play. He did a sick ass remix of Biggie Smalls Ten Crack Commandments. I made a quick escape to the bed room to change. I combed out my wrap, applied a little mascara and some Mac lip gloss in Bitch Red to compliment my shoes. Flora by Gucci was my choice of fragrance for this evening. It was one of the gifts T-Roy brought for me. He told me that he remembered me mentioning that I wanted it after smelling a sample of it in my latest subscription of Elle Magazine. I decided on the tear drop Cartier diamond earrings that he bought also. T-Roy barred no expense and he showered me with nothing less than the best of everything. He paid special attention to my body language. When we were together all I had to do was point to something that I admired and it would be delivered next day to the office. The sound of my intercom system snapped me out of my revere.

"D'Sire some of your guest are here." Sasha sang in the distance.

"Sash could you please buzz them in." I yelled back. He said something sarcastic but I couldn't quite make it out over the music. Monica and her husband Rob were the first to arrive followed by T-Roy's DJ, Shawn. Shawn brought a few heads with him two of them I recognized off the rip they were Trust and Project Pete from the rap group Lawful Villains. They had one of the hottest CD's out. Anyone who was someone stayed banging their music either in the crib or when they were out and about. I had two copies. One I coped the first week it dropped, the second came from T-Roy so I kept one on deck and the other in the car on blast.

"Oh my God D'Sire you are killin that Alexander MC Queen original." Angel said.

"Thanks Angel."

"See I told your ass that bitch had taste." I heard Sasha say as the two headed towards the balcony.

"Help yourselves to anything you want." I announced. More people poured in most of them I recognized from the office. Tyrell arrived and received mad love from both T-Roy and his DJ. He gave a sexy squint and licked his lips before approaching me. Damn this niggah is bold. I thought to myself, but at the same time hoping T-Roy did not peep his actions.

"Sup D'Sire, that article you wrote on the Battle Rappers was fire, thanks for the honorable mention."

"No problem." I casually said making my way to the kitchen. Tyrell followed close and grabbed my arm.

"Tyrell what the fuck are you doing?" I whispered pulling from his grip.

"Damn baby it's like that. It was all good a couple days ago when you were riding this dick."

"Yea but you know T-Roy is here and now is not the time."

"Then why the fuck you aint been answering my phone calls?"

"Listen Tyrell, I never promised you anything. We just fucked. I was tipsy as hell and feeling a little lonely and it just happened."

"Oh word D. So basically what you saying is that you used me and now you want us to pretend as tho it never happened. Aight I got you. I wonder how my mans would feel knowing that he wifing up a straight ass hoe."

"Tyrell you need to slow your fuckin roll on some real shit. I already done did my homework on you. Hey aren't you on parole? Did you tell your PO about the show you just did in New York? Or shall I send him a copy of the DVD I don't give a fuck what you tell T-Roy, go ahead Tyrell I have nothing to lose but you do." He took a step back.

"Fuck you, you crazy bitch." He vehemently spat.

"You gonna get yours." He damned there knocked Sasha down as he stormed from the kitchen.

"Oh no he didn't just bump me and didn't excuse himself." A look of concern washed over him. D'Sire honey are you alright? Did that bitch ass niggah do anything to you? Because I will forget that I'm a lady and straight rock his ass to sleep. Just say the word girl." I laughed at Sasha in an attempt to mask my true emotion.

"I'm straight Sash we were just discussing the piece I wrote on the Battle Rappers and he said something about misplacing his cell phone."

"Well if that motha fucker get it twisted just let me know girl."

"No need for violence Sasha dear everything is fine I promise." Sasha sucked his teeth.

"Alrite bitch if you say so."

## Chapter 24

"What's up Jamal I thought Dee Dee was coming."

"She had to pick up her cousin Nee Nee from the airport so she asked me to scoop you. Her cousin's man be beating her ass so she gonna be staying with Dee Dee's moms until she get on her feet."

"Yea but my pass is only for six hours. Will she be back in time?"

"I don't see why not she left over an hour ago. Don't worry D'Sire I got you, she left a big box stuff for you at the crib and she told me to make sure you take what you want and the rest she's going to give to her cousin. Let's go get something to eat and then we will stop by the house." I reluctantly agreed. Jamal took me to my favorite pizza spot, Captains where the buttery crust and oozing blend of cheese and sausage tantalized my taste buds in an erotic dance across my tongue. My senses heightened as I closed my eyes and took a bite. When I opened them I caught Jamal staring. It made me feel uncomfortable. "Damn D'Sire only you could make eating pizza into an art form."

"What's that supposed to mean?" I asked curious to what he would say.

"I'm just saying if I were to turn on my TV and saw you eating that pizza the way you just did I would run on foot to get to the restaurant because you made it look just that good, real talk." I was flattered but was careful not to show it. Although I've been around Jamal on several occasions I've never noticed the scar above his right eye and it was something odd about his demeanor that secretly turned me on.

"What happened to your eye Jamal?"

"Huh?" He blankly stared.

"Right here." I said as I leaned over the table and lightly stroked the raised jagged line.

"Oh I got grazed by a bullet when those niggahs killed Trent."

"Oh shit I didn't know you were with Trent when he got robbed."

"Yea it was so fucked up how they did my mans. I saw the whole thing as I was coming out the liquor store. He was arguing with one dude and another niggah came from behind and straight shot him point blank in the back of his head, he did not stand a chance. Then the niggahs had the nerve to frisk his body. They took his money and chain. When they caught sight of me they started bustin shots. My adrenalin was pumping through my body so fast I didn't even realize I was hit until I felt the sting of blood in my eyes. I've been having really bad headaches ever since that shit happened and the scene keeps playing over and over like a movie."

"Damn Jamal I'm so sorry you had to go through that." The energy in the space between us felt heavy and despondent. I felt his pain. The air was thick and tense as we shared silence. I was relieved when the friendly waitress placed the check on the table and asked if there was anything else that we wanted. The icy air that greeted us as we exited the restaurant felt refreshing to me as it made its way into my body instantly sending chills throughout that was welcomed. I could hear the revving of Jamal's midnight blue Suburban as he pointed the remote starter. He gently touched the small of my back as he led me into the massive vehicle before closing my passenger door. Just as he was about to put the truck in reverse I placed my hand over his.

"Jamal I am so sorry about Trent. I wish I never..." Before I could get what I wanted to express out his lips were upon mine and my seat was beginning to recline. I tried to resist but the sex demon that possesses me took over. I found myself kissing him back with a hungry vengeance, biting and sucking his bottom lip. Jamal's hand trembled as it clumsily fumbled the button of my jeans until finally it gave way granting him access to my sacred treasure. He slid my pants down this time with ease. Jamal gently caressed my inner thigh. My pussy began to pulse and I slid backwards in between the console into the roomy back seat of the cab. Jamal's eyes were locked upon of mine and he followed suit. My pussy dripped as Jamal cocked my red lace thong to the side and began to rapidly drill his tongue in and out of the sweet fat folds of it. I moved my hips in heavy rotation as I fucked the shit out of his mouth in a desperate attempt to cum. After all this was no love making session. My thighs shook as I reached my climax.

Jamal motioned me to turn around. He maneuvered his huge dick through the hole in the front of his boxers and zipper. He then slid his erection into me without protection. His moans were very audible as he expressed pleasure through clenched jaw and I held no shame, I actually felt vindicated as I bucked wildly reclaiming the throne that was rightfully mines in the first place.

"Damn D'Sire, this pussy is so tight, he said as his strokes became more intense, oh shit I'm about to bust he panted as he bore deeper in me. Jamal bit and sucked the side of my neck as he expelled his hot seed into me. We cleaned up with his son's baby wipes that were stashed in the glove compartment.

"You still got that blazin girl." He said with a smile.

"Yea so blazin that you went ahead, fucked and wifed up Dee the first chance you had." I replied clearly heated.

"Hold up yo it took a minute for me and Dee to fuck around. We both were going through some serious emotions with my best friend getting murked and you being in a coma and all, and to top it off all the rumors." His voice trailed off.

"Dee Dee nearly had a nervous breakdown behind that shit. It just happened, then in the mix of it all, my son was conceived. I didn't want to leave her alone to raise him by herself so I stayed." He explained.

"The whole timc you were gone I thought about you D'Sire. I even told Trent that you were the one, and after that shit happened to you I was fucked up for a long time. I aint gonna lie I even tried to visit you in the hospital, but they wouldn't let no one in but immediate family because you were a minor." Jamal's BlackBerry rang.

"Hey baby. Yea she's right here we just finished getting something to eat, and now we bout to head to the crib." Jamal handed me the phone.

"She wants to speak to you."

"What's up girl?" I asked in an upbeat tone.

"Girl I don't think ima make it back in time before your pass runs out, traffic is at a standstill." Dee Dee said clearly aggravated.

"Aww man I was looking forward to seeing you today." I whined.

"No worries I'll make it up to you. I have to call you anyway, girl I got some juicy shit to tell you."

"Oooo tell me now." I wined.

"I can't, I'll tell you later let me talk to Jamal."

"Alright hold on." I handed Jamal back his phone.

"Love you too bae." I heard him say before disconnecting. The feeling of jealousy creped upon my heart but was careful not to express it because I did not want to fuck up what I had going on with Jamal. My motives were covert beyond measure.

## Chapter 25

"Ooooo girl you rockin that shit!" Renee' exclaimed as Latoya modeled her new red and black lace negligee', that she copped from Victoria Secret.

"You aint seen nothing yet." Latoya said while snapping the black garter straps to her fish net thigh highs.

"Yo bitch, you about to straight have that niggah going insane!" Renee' shouted.

"Now turn around. Baamm! That's what I'm talking about. Yo ass look like a basketball in that shit girl you is most definitely killin em." Latoya threw her head back in hysterical laughter.

"Yea I am." She agreed after calming down. She admired her curves in the full length mirror.

"So bitch you never told me what this niggah had in store for you tonight. You been acting all secretive for the last couple of weeks and shit." Renee' expressed showing attitude.

"Because Nae you got a big mouth, you know you can't hold water." Latoya answered. Renee' drew in a long suck between her teeth and slit her eyes.

"What you mean I can't hold water?"

"All the shit we be doing together. I aint never told nobody." She said in defense.

"I'm not talking about that, I'm just saying you like to run your mouth to your man and you know how close he and Tyrone is. Just like the time when I told you not to say nothing about the condo, and what did you go do? Tyrone cussed me out for weeks' bout that shit. It will surely get back and I'm not taking a chance. I need him to know that he can trust me, tonight just may be the night I've been waiting for since I bagged this niggah last summer and I do not want to fuck it up because I couldn't keep my mouth shut."

"Bitch let me find out you about to be a married hoe."

"See that's the shit I'm talking about already jumping to conclusions. Shut up and help me pick out a pair of fuck me stilettos so I can get ready to go." Hearing that made me look up from my composition book.

"What the fuck you looking at bitch?" Latoya vehemently spat. I smiled inward and continued to write. This bitch had no clue what was in store for her. Renee' and Latoya continued to play dress up, so consumed by their world of false securities of material wealth that they didn't notice me leave, destination Rosedale Lane. It just so happened that today was orientation for school and staff was already aware so it was easy for me to acquire an extended pass. I signed out and hailed a cab. I opted out calling Re'mee because he would surely ask me a hundred and one questions and over all I was better off with a stranger who wouldn't be able to place me in the area. The ride seemed eternal as the ribs in my chest rattled void of rhythm to the beat of a cold palpitating heart. I began to hyperventilate in silence.

"Let me out right here." I blurted out. The cab suddenly came to a screeching halt. The meter read eighteen dollars and fifty-three cents. I handed the overweight cabbie a twenty- dollar bill and busted my way out the door into the freezing night that waited. Only two and a half blocks away but it was cold as hell. I pulled on the black scully and tugged on my North Face parka extra tight as I held conflict with the raging wind that shot icy particles down my throat every attempt I made to breathe. After what seemed like eternity, I finally spotted the complex. I've cased the area several days ago so I took a little short cut through a path I discovered that led straight to Latoya's front door. The key was still in its spot, underneath the brand new welcome mat. I reached for it with a gloved hand and opened the door then returned the key to its respective place. I then locked the door from the inside. My skin began to slowly burn as it thawed out one section at a time, first beginning with my hands. When my eyes finally adjusted to the darkness of the room, I could faintly see the layout of the stylish yet empty crib. The shit was hot to deff, and I wondered how a ghetto bitch such as Latoya could become so fortunate to receive such a lavish gift. The answer then came to me, she had to be loved. I was now having second thoughts and was about to leave, but the soft click of the front door lock stopped me in my tracks, and I didn't have time to hide.

"Tyrone is that you baby?" I was silent and stood still, unable to breathe or move. She came closer.

"Tyrone quit playing and answer me." She demanded and took a few more steps. She removed her trench coat.

"Tyrone I brought some candles, the electricity is supposed to be on Tuesday." She said this time striking a match. Our eyes locked.

"What the fuck are you doing in my house, you freak ass bitch?"

"Where the fuck is my man?" Latoya lunged at me and without thought my hand was wrapped around the bottle that I had stashed in my coat pocket and the contents were spewed upon her.

"Oh my God my face, somebody please help me!" She screamed. Her skin began to slide between her fingers, facial muscles exposed. The putrid smell of chemical and burning flesh filled the room as Latoya's face and the acid became one. I ran in the kitchen and grabbed a butcher knife out of the drawer and repeatedly stabbed her over and over in her chest. Her screams became gurgled as she choked on clotted blood. My hands trembled as I fumbled for the candle that Latoya dropped. I went back into the kitchen and turned on all four gas pilots including the oven then lit and placed the candle onto Latoya's bloodied lifeless body. Slowly it became engulfed in flames. I will never forget the look that her eyes gave me as they glazed over into their death slumber. An eerie silence fell upon the room and I ran out the condo as fast as I could without looking back. The next morning word spread like wild fire, everybody in the shelter was talking about the fire in Hamden and how supposedly they found a body in the apartment and so on. I continued to ear hustle throughout the day to see if Latoya's name was mentioned but to my surprise no one did. Renee' sulked around looking as if she would puke at any minute and we all huddled around the 32 inch Magnavox television in the rec room to watch channel 8 news.

"Detectives are keeping a tight lip and it has not been confirmed whether or not the badly burned remains are that of a man or woman. One thing that is certain is, this is a homicide." Several days had past when police and detectives swarmed the shelter and found the typed letter in Latoya's belongings. They picked up Tyrone on a warrant, and booked him on murder charges. Renee' could not accept the fact that her best friend was dead and had a nervous breakdown. She had to be committed to a mental facility. A grief consoler came to the shelter once a week to speak with us. I just went with the flow and silently thanked the universe that I got away with murder.

Chapter 26

2006

Things were starting to look up for me. Jamal and I were fucking on the regular, I was making straight A's and with my graduation being less than two weeks a way I was already bout to move into my first apartment, compliments of Jamal. He had no clue that my section 8 application had gotten approved and that I wouldn't have to dish out not one penny for the lavish one-bedroom luxury high-rise. It was a step down from where I really wanted to be but it would just have to do for now. I made a fake lease on the computer using a template from Staples, and Jamal gave me three thousand dollars for the security deposit and first month's rent, plus another five gees for an abortion which I pocketed. I figure a few more times doing this and I should be straight. Besides he was the one who insisted on fucking me raw and put the demands that I couldn't sleep with no one else, so a niggah had to pay. I couldn't wait to see what my graduation gift would be. I would have to trim this niggah as fast as I could because I had a feeling that Dee Dee was getting a little suspicious and I didn't know how much longer we would be able to do this. We've been fucking for three years strong now and I was catching feelings. I hated when I called and he would send me directly to voice mail, so I made him pay in other ways. I wasn't going to be a dumb ass bitch and let this niggah sit here and take care of her and turn around then fuck me for free. It was a damn shame just how many women would allow it, even worse take care of a niggah that wifed up the next bitch, hoping, praying that he would leave his girl. Their self-worth gone because it never happens. The type of chick that hustled backwards, dumb as fuck. Then wonder why they stay getting shitted on. I don't have any sympathy for no bitch especially a stupid one. I decided to give Jamal a key to my crib on the strength that he rendered all expenses, and I hadn't any plans on fucking that up anytime soon by allowing my emotions to get in the way. I knew what I was getting into the first moment I made the conscious decision to fuck him. I was totally aware of the risks that went along with being the side bitch, so I definitely had to remain vigilant and carefully calculate every move I made with Jamal because Dee Dee was no dummy and to keep it one hundred, she is the one who taught me everything I knew about the game and how to always come out the victor and if she had the slightest clue to what I was up to I don't have any doubt in my mind that she wouldn't rest until she made me pay. Jamal and I shopped at Trend Setters a high end contemporary home furnishing store where I had the privilege of picking out whatever my heart desired. I was blown away by all the luxurious one- of- a kind pieces that I knew would complement my apartment so well and my eyes lit up every time I would point to something and Jamal would motion to the smiling salesman to add to the long list of items I've already acquired. He didn't even blink at the $7,000 tab. Jamal simply handed over his Platinum American Express card then signed his life away. Delivery of my furniture wasn't set till the following week but I held nothing back as I allowed Jamal to slowly enter me anally and we fucked in that position on the floor in front of a candlelit fire place for over an hour. About a year ago when we first started having anal sex it was a painful bloody mess now his dick fits in my ass like a glove and I swear on everything the feeling is explosive especially when he cums inside it. Real talk I cannot get enough. Through deep moaning and heavy breathing, I could of sworn I heard a light tap at the front door and Jamal must of heard it too because we both froze. I started to get up but Jamal quickly gripped my arm tight cutting off its blood flow.

"What are you doing is you crazy girl?" Jamal spat as he whispered in my ear.

"What do you mean am I crazy Jamal somebody is at the door and why are you tripping nobody knows about this apartment yet but you and me anyway. I just wanted to look out the peek hole that's all." There was a knock again same like before but this time a little faster. Jamal's BlackBerry blared and he clumsily scuffled in the dark tripping over one of his Tim's to find his jeans so that he could quickly send the caller to voicemail. We sat completely still in silence because we both knew who the person was on the other side of my door. The knob rattled then turned.

"How could you two do this to me?" She screamed as she came busting through the door.

"I sat and watched y'all play me for over six months! It killed me to hold my composure while the two of you were in and out of every motel in town!" She exclaimed while reaching in her purse. Through dim light I could see the tear streaked face of a mad woman.

"Look at you two pitiful motha fuckas. Y'all scared now aint ya?" She asked exposing a pearl handled .25.

"I bet your wondering how the fuck I found out about yall lil fuck fest. Oh oh better yet how the fuck I got the key to the love pad. That's because niggahs are sloppy, straight up dogs they shit all over the place and don't know how to cover up they tracks." Dee Dee's words hissed hatred as she spoke. Then she turned to me.

"D'Sire I thought you were my lil sister I took care of you and this whole time you been scheming on my lifestyle. You aint shit but a dirty stankin ass hoe. I should have listened when my mother told me about you fuckin your uncle and having his baby, but I didn't want to believe that you were capable of such a nasty thing. She told me that I should leave you alone and that you would never be a good friend to me because you were damaged for life, and when she wanted to change her phone number I begged her not to. Why, because I believed in you and this is the shit you do to me?" Dee Dee began to hyperventilate, and her shoulders shook violently as she sobbed. I reached out to her.

"Back the fuck up bitch or I will blow your fucking brains out!" She screeched in a demonic manor.

"Baby please…just put the gun down we need to talk about this." Jamal said as he calmly took two steps towards her, hands extended.

"BACK THE FUCK UP!" Then a loud pop was the last I heard along with Jamal's piercing cry, and before my brain registered what had just happened Jamal was clutching his torso then collapsed to the floor. Dee Dee fell hard to her knees and dropped the gun. She laid her head on Jamal's chest and wept as he took his last breath. My legs felt like jello as they wobbled barely sustaining my weight and clumsily I made a fateful attempt towards the door.

"LOOK WHAT YOU MADE ME DO TO HIM YOU FUCKIN BITCH I'M GOING TO KILL YOU!" There are no words that can equate to the amount of fear that paralyzed me, but something within got me through the door right in time as bullets rang. I ran for my life, ass naked into the balmy night air. Car horns blared, and in the distance I heard one last shot. Deep inside I knew the recipient but never looked back. I continued to run feet bloodied from all the broken glass they've encountered. It felt as though I was having an outer body experience void of pain. I finally collapsed from exhaustion greeted by the steamy concrete that scraped my face. I laid there for a long moment unable to control my breathing unable to blink I was succumbed by trepidation I knew she was coming for me; they all were coming for my soul.

## Chapter 27

Present. Other than Tyrell trying to get it twisted my party was a sensation. My colleagues raved about it for weeks on end. Many cats from the industry came through to show me love and it never dawned on me just how well connected I truly was. T-Roy landed a new collaboration and my boss Monica was in networking heaven. I was living my highest ideal surrounded by great people. My past did not define me and I had reinvented myself to the point where my lies became my very own reality, and in my mind everything I've done was justified because it was necessary for my very own continued existence. I decided to leave work early today and it seemed as though everyone in the office felt the same way. My reason was so that I could beat the traffic on the way to the city. T-Roy had texted me earlier to come to Manhattan so I could give my approval on the building that he chose for Amnesia. I was quite flattered that he valued my opinion in such a way and butterflies gathered for a meeting in my stomach every time I thought of him. I was beginning to wonder if this is what true love really was supposed to feel like. I cleared my work station then turned off all the lights in the office. On the way to the car I decided to try Jazz again. To my avail still no answer. Hum mm, that's strange I thought. I've been blowing her phone up all day and she hasn't called back yet. Maybe Dominick is keeping her occupied. I smiled to myself at the thought. Even though I never had the chance to meet him I could just imagine how he must look in person just by the way she described him with his green eyes and dark skin and I understood why she hasn't answered her phone especially if he is laying pipe the way she says he does. My pussy became wet at the contemplation of us having a threesome and wondered if Jazzlyn had any idea just how often I fantasized about her and I having sex. In just a few hours I will be riding dick too and I could not wait. Traffic was brutal due to an I 95 South accident in Stamford and my aggravation level was at its peak because I was in such a rush that I skipped out on filling my tank so I was forced to turn off the AC to conserve what little fuel I had left and the heat felt more intense due to the slow crawl. Finally, after a three-hour drive that should have been one and a half, I arrived on 6 W 125th street in Manhattan. The towering grey wind chipped sand stone building bore signs of old age which made me second guess if I was at the right address but, according to the GPS I was. I dialed T-Roy no answer. Call it intuition but for some odd reason I felt a little nervous as though I was being watched. Reluctantly I entered. Once inside it was as if I stepped into a different world. From the looks it seemed as it did not require much work at all. It kind of reminded me Jay-Z's 40/40. My peep toe Prada stilettos clicked upon the decorative black & silver flecked flooring as I made my way across the massive room to the beautiful art deco glass mosaic bar where there was a stunning bouquet of blood red roses displayed. Although I found it oddly bizarre curiosity still allowed me to pick up the attached note card that revealed my name in a sexy gold cursive script and it read; follow the path, which I obliged. Although I was full of skepticism I followed the trail of rose petals that led me around a corner to an elevator. The bell chimed and the grand metallic doors parted. The sweet scent of flowers escaped its confines and lured me in with an invisible finger. The soft carpet of rose petals cushioned my feet which made me want to take my shoes off. I was caught somewhat off guard by the sudden jolt of the elevator when it began to ascend to the very top floor. Once the doors opened I slightly hesitated before continuing to follow the rose petal pathway. The view from the roof top terrace was amazing, nothing less than spectacular. There was a captivating reflecting pool with what seemed to be over a hundred floating tea lights. The Manhattan skyline, trendy settings and luscious vibe made me feel as though I was on top of the world, so I could only imagine how T-Roy's guest would feel once they experienced this ambiance. This was most definitely going to be the place to be for the privileged elite. I continued on the rose petal path with a feeling of uneasiness that I sensed at my core. My heart palpitated, I could feel the thumps leap in my throat and out of nervousness I bit my bottom lip. The sun angrily displayed bursts of blood orange and fuchsia undertones in brilliance as it began to inch its way behind the immense glistening Manhattan skyline. The intense burn was trance like and made me squint as I took in the beautiful scene of the massive buildings that reflected off the water like radiant sparks filled of wonder and mystery. Hearing my name called in the near distance caused my body to tense up.

It was T-Roy, I swiftly made way to where his voice came from and was met by a chorus of, "Surprise!" from several familiar smiling faces. My boss, coworkers, T-Roy's band, Jazzlyn, and a few well known cats from the music industry all gathered. I was caught off guard and everything began to move around me in a state of slow motion. Even though I was unable to process the scene that danced before me I was still overcome with excitement because I knew they were all here for me, but for what reason? It had to be for Oblivion I thought to myself.

"Hey baby, you are probably wondering what everybody is doing here." T-Roy stated over a mic.

"First and foremost I want to tell you that I am sorry for lying to you." My eyebrows narrowed, and someone chuckled in the distance.

"You're not here to put the final approval on my nightclub. In fact, I purchased it several weeks ago without telling you because I wanted everything to be perfect when I did this." T-Roy handed the mic to Sonnie and walked over to me. He got on one knee and presented the most stunning ring I have ever seen in my life. I was bedazzled by the radiant, emerald cut 15 carat Diamond surrounded by six rows of shimmering baguettes that iced out the platinum band they graced. I immediately clutched my heart and simultaneously the salty water began to flow from the wells of my eyes.

"D'Sire, I am so in love with you, and would be honored if you could make me the luckiest man in the world by becoming my wife." For what seemed like eternity I was stuck; speechless my tongue felt distended like it had just gotten pierced. I held my midsection and with a barely audible whisper I managed to squeeze out a yes. With a pregnant pause, time stood still as T-Roy slid the brilliant gems on my trembling finger.

"She said yes!" He exclaimed, and the crowd of onlookers went berserk.

"Congratulations to my brother from another mother T-Roy and his gorgeous wife to be, D'Sire on their engagement; now let's get this party started." DJ Enuff blared threw the mic. T-Roy took my hand and we broke away from the crowd to a sequestered candle lit VIP area. I was grateful to have some private time with him just so I could take all what just happened in.

"How did you pull this one off Troy without me finding out, especially with Sasha's big mouth?

"Well it wasn't easy, I had to do a lot of bribing when it came to him, I damned there promised everything but our first born for him to keep this secret."

"I bet, because Sasha loves to gossip and I know it had to kill him not to spill the beans." I said.

"Also I changed the name of the establishment to Club D'Sire; the custom signage is being delivered next week; and I hired Angel and Sasha to design the place, and of course Monica is already claimed rights to the exclusive." He said displaying that impeccable smile I love. I just could not accept as truth in my mind how my life has changed over this past year, how everything in my life seemed picture perfect. I felt like I cheated to get to where I was somewhat undeserving, yet entitled. Mixed emotions began to flood my space but I shook them off because this was my special night and I wasn't going to allow my self-sabotaging behaviors mess this up for me. To switch my state of mind I silently reaffirmed my self-worth and danced the night away with my husband to be.

## Chapter 28

Several weeks into our engagement T-Roy and I had planned on moving me out of my condo in CT. to his Sky rise in Manhattan. Most of my belongings I put on consignment. Good money was paid for my shit and no matter what jackpot I just hit I wasn't losing out. Everyone was looking solemn in the office because I put in my two-week resignation. I made the conscious decision to oversee Club D'Sire; plus, T-Roy purchased real estate in Manhattan for my new public relations firm. There was a lot of work to be done and the stress of trying to meet Monica's deadlines and my own endeavors just would not work. With me being as dedicated as I am to my craft, something would have to give. It's amazing how life could go from one extreme to the next. My convictions have never let me down, I have always been a firm believer in the concept that everything is attainable, and we as supreme beings can be do or have anything we so wish just as long as we put it out into the universe, next believe with all our heart mind and soul that whatever we asked for is coming, then let it go with the perceived notion that it is on its way to physically manifest itself into a delicious reality that is not meant to be questioned. I've been practicing the art of manifesting my desires my whole entire life and didn't realize it until I came across a precious gem in a book called Harmonic Wealth; written by my favorite author. In this book I discovered the key that opened my mind beyond what words can explain. It teaches about the metaphysical law of attraction and how to make it work for you. I've also learned that sometimes we attract what we don't want by default, so now I try to be more mindful of the words that I speak. Everything on the outside is a mere reflection of what is going on the inside. I know that's how I was able to bag T-Roy and have the immoderate lifestyle that I am now living. I feel blessed, favored in a way beyond a reasonable doubt. News of our engagement spread like a disease in a body with a compromised immune system, and paparazzi trailed my every move. It was overwhelming, the constant flash of the cameras kept me in a daze and I was beginning to catch headaches. They would camp outside of my condo and chase me on the highway. The only time I felt some sense of peace is when I was in the confines of T-Roy's sky rise abode. Even if I decided to stay, it would be difficult to live here under these stressful conditions, I was physically and emotionally drained, I had no choice but to leave Connecticut because I felt like a captive in the state that I loved so much. My life had significantly changed and I knew what I was getting into the moment I signed up to be with Troy. My cell phone rang; it was Jazzlyn.

"Hey girl what cha getting into today?" she asked all upbeat.

"Nothing, I think I'm going to hibernate in my crib until I move in with Troy." I said using my best doomsday impression.

"Well I have some great news home girl, and you have no choice but to say yes or else I'm going to have to kidnap your ass myself and throw you in the trunk." Jazzlyn joked. There was a long pause and I managed to let out a fake laugh.

"H e l l o Jazz, I'm listening."

"Oh my bad just wanted to know the level of your interest." She teased.

"Come on Jazzlyn stop playing you have no clue to how stressed out I am. This whole wedding thing, the sudden fame, I feel as though I'm losing my sense of self." I wearily expressed. Tears of silence streamed and Jazzlyn must have sensed the tension because her whole tone changed.

"Aww man D'Sire I'm so sorry girl, your right I didn't have a clue." She expressed in a concerned tone.

"It's not your fault Jazz. It's just that for the past few weeks my life has been turned upside down."

"Girl I have just the cure for the paparazzi blues." Jazz said with a smile I could feel through the phone.

"Dominick just purchased a vacation cottage on a remote five-acre island in Alexandria Bay, New York. Oh my god D'Sire it's to die for! I'm talking about 5500 sq. feet, six bedrooms three and a half bathrooms. Not to mention all the amenities you could ever dream of, including a fully stocked wine cellar and on premise massage therapist. He just closed on it yesterday and told me that I could come and go as I please; Girl I got the keys!" she shouted into the receiver. I heard something smash in the background.

"Oh shit D'Sire I just knocked my damn wine off the dresser, let me know what you think; I have to clean this glass up before fluffy gets cut. I'll call you right back." She hurriedly said, and disconnected. Damn a weekend getaway is just what my mind, body and soul has been calling for. I know T-Roy won't have a problem with me going either because he's too busy preparing for his upcoming Bedroom Candy tour. No need to think about anything. Alexandria Bay here I come.

## Chapter 29

"Girl I am so excited about this little getaway." I said as I put the last of several luggage into the back of Jazzlyn's white Range Rover.

"Damn D'Sire you sure you coming back? Looks like you have your whole life in them bags." Jazzlyn joked.

"I messed around and didn't start packing until last night and you know I'm still in the process of moving so I wasn't sure of what to take. The movers are still in and out so I didn't want to leave nothing behind that I may need; and didn't you say that this cabin was on some kind of island? Shit I brought my survival kit just in case. Jazzlyn threw her head back and laughed.

"Yea its upstate New York, you're going to love it because, we literally have to park and take a boat to reach it. We got lucky because the previous owners threw theirs in with the house, now Dominick doesn't have to buy one. You didn't tell anybody you were going did you." Jazzlyn asked.

"Hell no, but I did tell Troy that I needed to take a weekend sabbatical to get into character for this new novel that I'm writing. He understood because I've done it in the past, Jazz I really just want to relax and not have to worry about anyone or anything."

"Amen to that girl." She said and gave me dap. The ride was a little over five hours and just as Jazzlyn said we took a small boat to the island. The thick smell of algae lingered in the air, and it felt as if it was sticking to my skin. The humidity was brutal, thankfully I decided on wearing the curly look. Once on the island I immediately fell in love, I felt as though I have stepped into a page of one of my favorite novels. It was gorgeous. The lush land scape took me into a world that did not exist in the physical. The trees formed a canopy to hide whatever secrets they knew, and the birds displayed marvelous colors amplified in bright greens, reds and yellows. The island reminded me of Jurassic park. The highlight of this private getaway was the grand yet idyllic cottage that stood only steps away from the lake. The whole outer structure was composed of red cedar logs, and two yellow pine rocking chairs sat side by side upon a gorgeous wraparound porch. The aromatic wood instantly made me feel received, and anticipation swelled in my chest, and I was fanatical to see what the inside would bring. The interior was stellar, with its beautiful rustic walls and high beam celling that soared. The open floor plan showed off a stainless steel gleaming chef's kitchen. The spiral staircase ascended into the master loft which over looked the living room.

"This is where we're going to sleep D'Sire, trust me on this one; the rooms are so spaced out that we won't get to see each other if we don't." I put my shoulder bag on the grand king size Italian canopy bed. Every room we entered seemed more spectacular than the next. I made a mental note to ask T-Roy to get us a private vacation home as soon as I got back but on a much smaller scale. Speaking of I need to call him to let him know that I made it here safe. I thought to myself. Damn no signal.

"Jazz I need to use your cellphone girl; I'm not getting any signal on mine."

"Look by the side of the bed, mines is charging; it was completely dead." I tried to dial on hers.

"Shit; girl do you have a landline?"

"Yea and no, the previous owners already had it shut it off, and Dominick hasn't switched over his info yet to the phone company. Girl chill everything's going to be alright; I thought you wanted to escape from it all anyway."

"No it's not that it's just that I wanted to let T-Roy know that I made it here in one piece that's all." I said still trying to dial out. "Oh well fuck it, I'll just try again later." "What do you have to eat in this joint, a bitch is starving?"

"Actually I was about to make us some lemon pepper salmon steaks on the grill and a nice chef salad. I made sure Dominick stocked up on food, and liquor as well, just in case a bitch got stranded on this shit." That made me laugh.

"Girl you are so crazy for that one but I'm glad ya did, you know how black folks is about our food and liquor. We don't play when it comes to our shit, we can't sustain with one or the other trust and believe." I said with a slight neck roll.

"D'Sire guess what else I got?"

"What, a dildo?"

"No bitch something better than that."

"Shit I don't have a clue to what could be better than dick whether it's fake or not, Jazz." Jazzlyn reached in her Fendi purse and pulled out a sandwich bag of some high grade weed and a prescription pill bottle.

"Bitch what are those?" I asked pointing to the bottle.

"Girl this is the magic that's going to have us floating on cloud nine this weekend." She said with a sexy grin and wink.

"Where did you get those from?" I asked

"Sorry can't give up my source, but just know I have access to shit that the average person can't get." She said shaking the bottle.

"Let me find out you been jacking Dominick." Jazzlyn busted out laughing. "Oh my god, Jazz what if he finds out you been taking his shit?"

"Girl and if he do ill just fuck the shit out of him and make him forget about the whole damn thing." She said with a two finger snap.

"Chill girl I got this." She said with her lips puckered and a look that reeked confidence. Hearing that familiar phrase made me pause.

"What did you just say?" I asked.

"I said chill, why?"

"Nothing, I thought you said something else. I felt a little uneasy.

"Girl we came here to relax, ease up a little D'Sire." I enjoyed my first night on the island. We ate, smoked, and watched a slew of movies till we both fell out from exhaustion. I slowly awoke to the delightful smell of turkey bacon and eggs. For a long moment I just laid in the comfort of the plush memory foam mattress, listening to the soft patter of the lake's ripples hitting the rocks. It felt real ethical to sleep late without the worry of meeting the demands of the superficial world that I co-existed in. From a distance, I could have sworn I heard Jazzlyn talking to somebody just above a whisper; but I could not make out what she was saying I laid still allowing my senses to float together. It's not like it really mattered anyway just as long as I was able to call T-Roy. I'm pretty sure he's a little worried by now. God forbid if anything happened, he wouldn't have a clue how to get here. There were so many twist and turns and paths that we drove through that I totally lost all sense of direction myself. Jazzlyn told me that the place is so remote, that it can't even be picked up by GPS satellite. I freshened up in the adjacent bathroom, then made my way down the stairs.

"I can't wait till this shit is over and then we can be together forever." I overheard Jazzlyn whispered into the receiver.

"Hey girl." I chimed. Jazzlyn dropped her cellphone causing it to separate from its case.

"D'Sire you scarred the shit out of me!" She said scrambling for the device.

"My bad, I figured I could catch some of that good ole signal you been yapping on because my phone still won't pick up one."

"What makes you think that mine is working?" Jazzlyn's mood suddenly changed.

"Uhhh I just stood here and heard you talking."

"Bitch you haven't heard shit and since you so busy trying to sneak up on me, what the fuck exactly did you so call hear?"

"Jazzlyn you need to calm the fuck down because it's not that serious." I snapped back and crossed my arms. I didn't come all this way to deal with your bi polar ass, if that is the case then I could have stayed where I was at."

"You know what D'Sire your right, I apologize I've been trying to catch a signal all morning I'm just frustrated because It did pop in for a little while then poof it was gone right in the middle of our argument and Dominick got the last word in."

"He's not mad that we up here is he?" I asked.

"No girl he's upset because this was supposed to be our weekend getaway, and I told him that I wasn't going to hold my breath on it because every time we plan something together it never works out. His job is so demanding, his patients come first; and I was still heated so I snapped on you Please forgive me."

"Girl I understand, let's just forget this ever happened and keep it moving; we are supposed to be having the time of our lives not arguing with each other like two kids on the playground. With all these projects coming up, I don't know when I'm going to get a chance to do this again so I really want to make the best of it ok." I genuinely stated with my arms stretched out initiating a hug.

"So what's on the agenda for today?" I asked changing the subject quick.

"Well I figured we would explore the island a little, get some sun and eat whatever we want and not feel guilty for doing so."

"That sounds good and lord knows my ass could use me some sun. I've been hiding out in the house for so long trying to avoid the paparazzi that I lost my glow; I have to get my sexy back." I said scrunching my hair while looking at my pale reflection in the gold antique wall mirror.

"Hold on Jazz didn't you mention a masseuse?"

"Yes, she's married to the grounds keeper, Edwin. They live in the guest house in the back; we got real lucky with that package deal. They don't want much either, just room and board is suffice. They have the perfect jobs, especially that Mrs. Rosa, she added." After showering I decided on taking a little me time. I slipped away from the confines of the cabin into the spiny canopy of the pine trees that stood stern like London guards as if I needed a passcode to enter. The soft crunch of the tree's needles seemed to let off an aroma that reminded me of my childhood during Christmas with every step that I took. The stillness was somewhat eerie and felt as if someone was watching me, but I kept on moving towards the small clearing that was only a Just a few yards away and I could see what appeared to be the guest house. It was an exact replica of the main cabin but much smaller, and the grounds were not as kept. Weeds grew amongst the brightly colored begonias in the attempt to choke the life out of the tender beautiful bed of flowers. It just seemed oddly strange to me that the grounds keeper would not maintain this part of the property especially when he and his wife occupied it. I continued to walk the path that led me directly to the front porch of the guest house and lightly tapped on the door. No answer, so I tapped a little louder. I cupped my hands around the outer edge of my eyes in a faithful attempt to shield the sun's glare so that I could peer through the small filmy window. It didn't seem to me like anyone lived here at all the furniture was covered with tattered tarp, dust particles danced upon the stream of sunlight and there were spider webs everywhere. I was about to turn the knob and enter because I could have sworn I heard Jazz tell me that Mrs. Rosa and her husband lived here, but the sudden sound of my name being called made me divert.

"Maybe there is more than one guest house." I thought out loud. It wouldn't be farfetched because the island is pretty big and I didn't get a chance to see the whole thing yet. Fuck it ill just ask Jazzlyn when I get back, I'm pretty sure she knows what's up.

"Here I come." I sang and trotted back to our cabin.

## Chapter 30

"This fucking rain has been nonstop since this afternoon." I said peering out into the torrential storm. The heavy drops hammered at the window like fists of a mad man that wanted to break in."

"Yea I know, the previous owner warned us about how unpredictable the weather was out here. I remember Mr. Simmons saying something about one minute we could be outside enjoying the rays of sunshine in our boat and the next paddling our asses to shore." That statement made me giggle. Loud simultaneous thunderclaps had me about to jump out of my skin; and the lights began to flicker.

"Don't worry girl I got your back." Jazzlyn jokingly said, nudging me on my arm.

"I have candles for days on deck and plenty of firewood to cook with." I was beginning to get home sick.

"It's not that, I know we're straight it's just..." My voice cracked a little.

"It's just, I hope T-Roy isn't going crazy worrying about me, that's all."

"Girl, you just need to relax that's all. This little getaway aint going to hurt nobody, and besides D'Sire, the key to a long lasting relationship is not overcrowding one another. Just imagine all the blazing I miss you sex you two are going to have." She said as she disappeared into the kitchen. She came back with a candle, two glasses and a bottle of Steytler, one of my favorite red wines imported straight from South Africa. T-Roy had put me on to it when we first met, and I've been hooked on it ever since. She poured me a full glass and lit the glass encased candle. I didn't hesitate as I closed my eyes to take a nice long sip of the deep ruby fermented liquid. A slow smile curled across my lips.

"Here take one of these." Jazzlyn handed me one oblong blue pill.

"What's this?" I asked.

"Girl stop acting all scarred this is the same shit I showed you yesterday quit acting like a little bitch and just swallow it. Look, I'm taking one too." She tilted her head back and before I could protest, the pill disappeared followed by a swig of wine.

"It's just like taking an e pill but the legal kind. It doesn't get no better than this." I hesitated but followed suite.

"Now just relax D'Sire.' Jazzlyn and I smoked weed, conversed and drank more wine, even though she seemed to babysit hers. I wasn't sure if it was me or if the pill was starting to take effect but all of a sudden my body felt real cool yet hot at the same time. Jazzlyn stood up behind me and began to gently rub my shoulders. As she pulled me out of my tee shirt my titties bounced and nipples danced to the tune of erect. She then knelt directly on the floor in front of me and began softly planting kisses from my breast to my navel, my eyes flickered closed as I felt light headed and aroused all at the same time. She untied the string to my sweat pants and slipped her manicured fingers under the elastic of the waistband of my boy shorts into the juicy folds of my fat throbbing pussy. I scooted my booty on the edge of the chair so she could slip everything off because I surely knew what was coming next. Jazzlyn hoisted my legs on her shoulder and tongue drove my pussy ferociously first with short rapid darts, then long stroking in and out of my swollen lips in a hungry attempt to mouth fuck me. In the heat of passion, somehow she came up out of all her clothes and we ended up on the rug in a sixty-nine. I finger fucked her ass and sucked her sweet pussy like I owned it, and for that very moment it was all mine. I visualized for months about what this would be like and I didn't want it to end no time soon. Jazzlyn and I scissor fucked, the heat and pressure of moist pussy rubbing against each other made us simultaneously have multiple orgasms. Jazzlyn kissed me on my lips then proceeded to walk into the other room. I just laid on the floor and closed my eyes waiting for her return so we could go another round. Tomorrow was our last night on the island but if things continue as they were we might have to stay a few more days, I thought to myself with a smile. Sex was my weakness especially with a beautiful woman.

"Jazz, what is taking you so long?" I wined; parting my legs at the same time. My pussy lips immediately swelled to the gentle touch of my fingers as they gently stroked it. I grasped my budding nipple and softly rolled it back and forth between my pointer and thumb. My stroking became a little more intense and I bit hard on my bottom lip to try and contain the audible grunts and cries of ecstasy that escaped between my teeth. Jazzlyn returned, just in time to suck me off into oblivion. We fucked throughout the night as our symphony of moans became one with the storm. Soon after drifting off to sleep. Visions of me running into a wooded area flashed through my mind. Someone or something was chasing me. I knew it was close because I could feel the scorch of its hot breath stick to the sweat on my neck, and tree branches whipped across my face as I ran. I was terrified beyond measure. Whatever it was grabbed hold of me, tearing my flesh as its razor claws ran down my back. I tripped over a decaying root and landed on my knees. I quickly turned on my side and through tear blurred vision I could see the silhouette of what looked to me like a woman's face, and she appeared to be holding something in her hand. A sharp blow to the ribs sent the wind flying out of me, and I fell face down on to the wet ground. She put her knee into my back and I felt the pressure of what felt like a screw enter my back followed by a burning sensation that traveled throughout my veins. My blood curdling screams went unheard as crashes of thunder carried them away into the night. My body started tingling and I felt a tightening first in my chest then my throat started to close.

"Relax D'Sire, allow the drug to take effect. The more you fight the paralysis, the worst it will be." Said the familiar yet evil voice. She left me for several minutes and the stinging rain that pelted my face began to pool into the dip where my head laid. Water rose, entering my nostrils. I was still aware enough to know that I was drowning.

"Oh no bitch I am not through with you yet." Said the demonic voice, while yanking my head out of the water. She wrapped me in a white sheet she brought back and proceeded to drag me, faced down several yards. I heard the creaking sound of a door as it slowly opened. The woman grunted as she strained to drag the dead weight of my body up the three steps that led to the porch and into the cabin. Although my senses were compromised I could still smell the damp musky odor of the structure once we entered. My head banged onto the wood floor as the woman roughly tore the sheet from under me. I could not blink my eyes, and when she lit the candle the blurry image of a sadistic Jazzlyn appeared in front of me. I could hear her rummage through metal objects as they clanged together, and the sound of some sort of power tool approaching, followed by an eerie silence.

"D'Sire, if you could talk you probably would ask me; why is this happening? Well, I'll let you in on a little secret. I'm not who you think I am. Do you remember your best friend? The one who always looked out for you, the one who treated you like a sister?" she asked vehemently.

"Oh you don't remember?" she asked if I could talk back. She cocked her head to the side, blinking several times. I suddenly realized that this was real and that the drugs she fed to me earlier must have put me in a temporary dreamlike state. One tear slowly streamed my face and rolled off my chin. I felt betrayed.

"Do you remember Bitch?" She shrieked, as she removed a crinkled picture of Dee Dee, Jamal and their baby during much happier times from her pocket. She gapped open my mouth with her dirt smudged fingers and shoved the photo in. I couldn't fight, I could not breath. Next she injected me with an unknown substance and I immediately became one with darkness.

## Chapter 31

My eyelids rapidly fluttered open as I fought the sting of the sunlight that peered through the window of what seemed to be the cabin where the grounds keeper and his wife stayed. There was an excruciating pain throughout my whole entire body, especially my throat. I tried to move my hands to touch it but they were handcuffed to two metal links that came out of the floor. My body felt partially numb from whatever Jazzlyn injected me with the previous night, but I was determined to get the fuck off this island or die trying. I had no clue what so ever that my life was being plotted on the whole time I knew her.

The sudden rattle of the door knob made me jump and I instinctively shut my eyes in a desperate attempt to thwart her off, "Rise and shine bitch." She sang as she came busting into the cabin. I laid still as a church mouse.

"Oh come on D'Sire do you really think you could trick me by fake sleeping? I'm not new to this, in fact Dominick doesn't exist. I'm the real Dr. I lost my license due to a malpractice lawsuit, because I accidently administered too much anesthesia to a patient, and in turn served twelve years for manslaughter. That's where I met my lover, my wife Dee Dee."

"Matter of fact after I kill you, I'm going to turn myself in so that we could be together forever. You see D'Sire you can't go around fucking people's lives up with the expectation that Karma will let you slide; it doesn't work like that honey." I vowed to revenge Jamal's death on Dee Dee's behalf so that her soul could be saved." She spat in my ear. I slowly opened my eyes.

"That a girl." She said cocking her head slowly side to side while twirling a stiff lock of my bloody mangled hair around her finger, and in one sudden move she tore it from the follicle. I tried to scream but no sound came out. Jazzlyn placed a long handled mirror in front of me and all I could do was stare, in revulsion first at the black and purple raised bruises that disfigured my face, then my eyes shifted to the gaping hole in my neck from which a bloody plastic tube stuck out.

"Now don't you get all riled up D'Sire, all I did was perform a little tracheotomy on you. After I injected the lidocaine and fentanyl into the outer membrane of your spinal cord I noticed that your blood pressure started to decline, due to the paralysis of your vocal chords. Instead of crying you should be thankful that I'm allowing you to breathe for now you ungrateful bitch.'' Jazzlyn spat as she lit a cigarette. She took a long drag then exhaled the white cloud of smoke through her nostrils, then began to pace the room and whisper rapidly. My eyes followed as she went back and forth talking to the imaginary person who seemed to walk with her. Suddenly she darted over to me, and without warning, she ashed her cigarette into the tender bruised flesh of my face, right below my left eye. As I screamed in silence, spurts of air mixed with a bloody mucus exited the tube and splattered onto the mud stained sheet that concealed my body.

Jazzlyn's cell phone rang. "Oh, I forgot to mention." She pulled out a small black device out of her pocket. "This is why you could not make or receive calls." After a long pause she began to speak.

"Hi sweetheart, yes everything is going according to plan, uh huh; well as a matter of fact she is, you can tell her yourself; although I must warn you, she won't be able to talk back." Jazzlyn hit the speaker button, and held the phone to my ear.

"I'm going to make this quick because my call is being recorded. I bet you thought I was dead. Surprise bitch I'm still around; but unfortunately you're not so lucky. You see D'Sire, I've been planning your demise for the past seven years. I treated you nothing less than a sister and the whole time your intentions were covert and conniving. I set you up, by using Jazzlyn to befriend you, so you would know how it feels to be deceived by the very person who is supposed to love you." Tears streamed my face.

"I want you to physically experience the emotional pain you put me through, and I will make you pay with your life for the life you stole from me D'Sire, because I am dead now, not only did I lose my freedom bitch, I lost my son, and everything else I've ever loved. My family won't even bring him up here to see me because of what you've done." Her voice cracked. To hear these words, she expressed not only cut me like a knife but, hurt me to my core, and not only were they so true but she will never get a chance to hear how truly sorry I really am.

"You have one minute remaining on this call." Said a mechanical voice through the speaker. Jazzlyn left the room, and shortly returned, eyes red with fury.

"Do you know how much it hurts for me to hear my baby cry about what you've done to her and for me not being able to console her?" Jazzlyn's whole body shook and her eyes rolled back in her head like a demon possessed.

"Bitch I'm going to make you suffer before I take your life." Her breath reeked hatred as she bent directly over me. Dry spit foamed from her mouth as she hissed.

"By now you should be regaining all feeling back to your body." Jazzlyn was right, before she mentioned it my body felt numb, and now that I am consciously aware that it's not, the pain hit me like a brick all at once, and my body began to tremor violently. Jazzlyn threw her head back, the roar of laughter that emitted from her was unnaturally sinister as she roughly snatched the sheet off of me. I struggled to lift my head up a couple of inches above the ground. Jazzlyn nails dug deep into my scalp as she pulled me up into full view by my hair, and my mouth gapped open in horror at the Carnage that displayed itself in front of me. More spurts of bloody mucus flew from the tube as I tried to force sound from where my larynx once was.

"Looking for these?" Jazzlyn sang as she held each one of my mangled legs above her head, they appeared to be grey in color due to the life force being cut off from them. Clotted blood slowly dripped like thick sap from a maple tree. The pain was unbearable that I welcomed my own death.

"Mann, you sure are a leaker, don't you just love the way I singed the stubs so they almost match, considering what I had to go through to do it." She casually said tossing my dead torn limbs to the side.

"You lost so much blood last night that I was afraid I was going to lose you and that you wouldn't be awake to witness the grand finale." I began to drift in and out of consciousness. Visions of my life began to slowly dance before me, the sweet smell of my grandmother's perfume, permeated the room. I saw me as teenager getting teased by Tyreek, and Dayshawn at the bus stop, along with me and Dee Dee on our shopping spree at the mall.

"You will always be my little sister D'Sire." I heard her say clear as day.

"Wake up bitch this shit isn't over." Jazzlyn shrieked as she water logged me. I heard 5 loud pops and several seconds later felt various sharp pains from the nail studs that pierced my stomach. Blood began to rise into my chest cavity and I could feel myself drowning in my own blood. My eyes were wide open as I gagged, and my last breath was snatched from me soon as Jazzlyn slit my throat in one motion. This time there was no warm misty white light to carry me, there were no peaceful feelings that made my soul flutter, and only terror consumed my being as I slowly descended into the dark trenches of what I now realized was my very own hell. In the distance I saw a dark figure with its arms stretched.

“D’Sire I’ve been waiting for you.” He whispered in a snake like manor, and a wicket smile crept across my lips because finally, I was reunited with my uncle, this time for all of eternity.

Made in the USA
Columbia, SC
26 May 2024